PACO SAVES THE DAY

PACO SAVES THE DAY
BOOK 1

NICHOLAS TURNER

Artwork by Luciano Fleitas

https://www.artstation.com/lucianofleitas

Typography by Simon Escobar

Instagram.com/masterlootdg

Editor: Melissa Stone

azuredragonpress.net

No AI was used during any part in the creation of this book

For Sam

Who always told me not to beat the shit out of Paco every chance I could

I'll never stop wandering. And when the time comes to die, I'll find the wildest, loneliest, most desolate spot there is.

EVERETT RUESS

CHAPTER 1

"REALLY? That's what you do? Film yourself feeding raccoons and uploading them to YouTube?" Helena said with disdain.

"Uhhh, yeah? Why is that such a problem?" I asked.

"It's just such a stupid thing to do for a living."

"I don't see how. I enjoy it."

"You just have nothing going for you." Her words hung in the air as we sat in the restaurant. "Do you have any dreams or aspirations? Anything?"

"I'd like to be a writer one day. Or maybe just travel. I have a few ideas for some books, but I'm not really sure where to start," I replied. I knew this wasn't going to last long.

I watched as Helena rolled her eyes. "Great, another social media star who thinks they can just write a book and become rich and famous."

There was a hatred starting to burn in my chest for my date. A self-righteous, holier-than-thou bitch who thought she was above everyone else just because she had a job that could turn into a career.

"You know, artists are what keep the world hopeful," I said.

"Save me the spiel. We can just eat and go our separate ways." She buried her face in the menu.

I watched as our waiter came over with our drinks. I had gotten an old-fashioned with Bulleit Bourbon. She had gotten a Cosmo with well vodka. Years of working in restaurants told me all I needed to know about her. She sucked. I should've seen the red flag before she went on her tirade.

"Are you guys ready to order?" he asked.

"You know, I think I'm done here," I said. "Here's twenty for my drink, and another twenty for you. The blonde menace across from me can pay for herself." I handed the man the green bills and stood up.

I looked down at Helena, who now looked utterly dumbfounded.

"No, no, no. I didn't mean the things I said. I was more just shocked by what you do," she said as her face turned bright red in embarrassment.

"I'm good." I didn't like conflict. I didn't want to argue or defend myself. Not to some random girl I started talking to on one of those stupid dating apps. "Besides, I have better things to do." I threw on my black zip-up jacket and made my way towards the door.

"Like go home and feed your stupid raccoons for YouTube?" she yelled.

"Those 'stupid fucking raccoons' have more personality than you do. And yes. That's why I've made more money in the last six months than you've made in the last ten years," I shouted as I flipped her off and walked out the door.

I was annoyed as I got into my car and sped home. It wasn't the nicest car on the block, but it was reliable. Sure, I could afford something way more expensive, but what's better than a 1991 Mazda Miata? Nothing. They're perfect. The best car Mazda ever produced. Mine was wrapped in matte black vinyl . Originally, it was red, but I wasn't a fan of the bright color. I also replaced the headlights to have purple LED halos. Yeah, I'm that guy. But, like I said, it was the best car ever made. And I stand by that. I didn't need to spend hundreds of thousands on a supercar. Just me, my Mazda, and my 'stupid fucking raccoons.' I sighed as I sped along the back roads and monologued to myself. The roads wound tightly, but that's what made this car so great. I could floor it, stick to the road, and just *go*.

I pulled into my driveway, got out of my car, and went through the gate to my backyard.

"Paco!" I shouted as I saw that fat, round raccoon sitting in my yard waiting for me. "Where are the others?" I asked.

He rubbed his paws together and just chirped in response. "I'll be right back," I said as I slid the glass door to my kitchen open and flicked on the camera in the window. He was already in frame. *Perfect.*

I grabbed a pack of hot dogs from the fridge and English

biscuits from the counter before I went back out. I hated calling them biscuits; they were more like cookies, but I tried to respect the culture. Paco loved them. I flicked on my monitor, which was attached to the outside of my house behind a sheet of plexiglass. It allowed me to read the comments without having to look at my phone.

"Hey guys, it's me again," I said as I walked into the camera's view. The livestream had already started, and my viewer count was close to ten thousand. "Chris here to show you my visitor for the night. It seems only Paco came as winter is about to set in. I'll probably start seeing less and less of them as time goes on. But anyway, I got hot dogs and biscuits." I raised both packages into view before I turned to walk towards Paco. He came *running* when he saw them.

"This guy really does love biscuits," I said as I sat in the chair on my back deck. "Not the biggest fan of hot dogs, but I'll keep them here just in case we get any other visitors."

Paco jumped into the chair next to me, sat on his ass, and started rubbing his paws together.

"Okay," I said, "only because you asked so nicely." I handed over a biscuit, and he started munching on it immediately.

I slid off my shoes and sat there talking to the camera. Overhead, helicopters whizzed by with spotlights. It completely ruined the video, but I let the livestream continue.

"Bigman69, hi. Yes, I have names for all the raccoons who come to visit. I can tell the difference. Me and Paco here have a special bond. He's been in my house a few times, but he doesn't do it often. Sometimes I can coax him into the kitchen, but it usually takes a few of these biscuits." I raised the box and shook it. Paco looked up to me and rubbed his hands together again even though he was still munching away.

"Nice to see you again, Angelofdusk."

"Mods, can you start banning people who are just going to start using slurs. Come on, I pay you guys for this."

I was answering and fielding questions like it was second nature.

The helicopters above became more frequent as the livestream went out. More than once, I saw Paco look up at the noise.

"It's okay, buddy," I said as I brushed my hand across his head. That seemed to quell his fears. He rubbed his hands together again, and I handed over a third biscuit.

One of the lights overhead stopped and shone down on us. I put my hand

instinctively around Paco so he would stay with me. The bright light had completely ruined the shot. It got brighter, and I felt a tingling sensation in my stomach that made me want to throw up.

I blinked multiple times trying to understand what had just happened. I was outside with Paco. We were livestreaming. Now, I wasn't outside. I was somewhere else, surrounded by metallic walls and computer screens glowing with neon. I tried to stand up. As I pushed off the ground, my legs gave out. My equilibrium was off. I looked to my right. Paco was still beside me, his biscuit on the floor.

"Am I tripping? Did that bitch drug me?" I looked forward to see if my camera was still there. Nothing. Just a vast room with a bunch of computers. There was a noise behind me. I spun on my knees.

In front of me stood three gray figures. Their legs were long and slender. Their eyes, bulbous. Their mouths, tiny little slits in huge heads.

"What the fuck?" I whispered before I threw up on the floor in front of me and blacked out.

CHAPTER 2

I WOKE up strapped to a table. All of my limbs were strapped down like I was a starfish. There was a coolness on my right arm. I craned my neck and saw a strange, dark silver sleeve. It ran from my wrist to my elbow. Paco was strapped to a similar table next to me. A small bracelet was visible on his front leg. The skin on his scalp was pulled back, and I saw a machine drilling silently into his skull. It suctioned the blood away as it worked.

"Where am I?" I asked no one in the room. "I swear to God, I have to be dreaming." I threw my head back harder than I should have.

An electronic sound came from my left. I turned to look as three alien figures strolled through the door. I felt my blood pressure drop, my head get dizzy, but this time, I didn't pass out. Probably because I was lying down.

"Who are you?"

They all looked at each other and muttered something unintelligible before turning back to me. They crossed the room. One of them stepped forward and started poking at the sleeve on my right arm. A screen lit up neon green.

"Stop touching me! Let me go! Let him go too!" I shouted as I looked over at Paco.

"There we go. Now you should understand us," the one who toyed with the sleeve spoke.

This time, being prone didn't help. "What the fuck?" I whispered before the world went black again.

———

"Hey! The stupid human is waking up!"

I blinked, and the room came back into view. I was still strapped to the table. I looked to my right. Paco was gone. The table was empty.

I felt like I was about to be killed by whatever these things were. They reminded me of the grays I had seen watching all those documentaries on Roswell. Each of them spoke quickly, but I didn't comprehend a word they were saying. My mind was racing. I swore to myself it was just a bad dream, or a bad trip from what Helena had snuck into my drink.

One of the aliens came over and stood by my head so I didn't have to strain my neck anymore looking at them.

"Listen, it's fine. You're safe now," it said.

"Let me go!" I shouted. Spit came from my mouth and landed on its face. It wiped it away with its long, four-fingered hand.

"Disgusting," it mumbled.

"I saw what you did to Paco!"

"He's fine. Look," it said as it pointed to the far wall. Paco was sitting on a chair eating biscuits. He waved. No, like, he really fucking waved at me. Almost as if he recognized me.

"I don't understand. Oh God, I think I'm going to pass out again," I said.

"Nope," the alien replied as he pulled a syringe out from under the table and jabbed it into my arm. My heart raced like I was on enough adrenaline to single-handedly kill Genghis Khan and his entire army.

"Okay, okay, okay," I said. "I'm dreaming. Or tripping. I'm surrounded by aliens, and Paco waved at me like he knows me. That's fine. Close your eyes. You've done stupid shit before. You'll be fine. Just breathe," I repeated to myself as I tried to ground myself.

"Yeah, no. You're on our spaceship. You're safe here. Your world was being attacked by orcs. We intervened and tried to save as many of you as possible. We declared war on them in the process. Your world is burnt to a crisp, which is most unfortunate, but you're alive! That's gotta count for something!" the alien said cheerfully.

I tried to understand what had just been said to me. Orcs? Abducted? War? I closed my eyes and squeezed tight. *Okay, just play along. Play along with the bad trip.*

"Okay. If my planet is gone, how many people did you guys save with this ship? How many ships are there? Why me?"

"Well... you see. We saved only you and that

wonderful friend of yours. He's really a delight! Some of our other ships were able to save a few as well, but we jumped out of the galaxy once we got you. The orcs auto-locked onto our position the second we jumped in. We grabbed you because it was convenient. I wish we could have saved more." The alien looked down to the floor.

"Okay, okay," I sighed. "So what're you gonna do with me now? Probe me? Use me in experiments?"

"Heavens, no! We're going to take you to our home, of course! You're our guests. We've always tried to make contact over the years, but the Council had a lot of red tape about it. And we never really figured out the language barrier until recently. Now you have that new fancy device on your arm. It does a lot, but we can get to that later. If I let you go, will you attack me?"

"No," I said. "I will not attack you."

"Promise?"

"Yes."

"Like, really, *really* promise?"

I sighed. "Yes, I really, *really* promise not to attack you." The alien was more like a toddler or a girlfriend who just wanted reassurance.

"Okay, good. Cause if you attack me, I'm going to have to fight back, and I really don't want to." It clicked a button, and my arms and legs were immediately freed.

"Chris!" a voice said.

I sat up, and Paco was running towards me.

"Chris, Chris, they have biscuits here!"

"What the fuck is going on?" I raised my hands and rubbed the sides of my head.

Paco was now on the table I had been strapped to. He struggled for a moment as he tried to jump and grab the edge to pull himself up. I watched as he slipped and plopped onto the floor. He tried again, this time making it.

"Are you really talking?" I asked.

"Yes, Chris. They did quick surgery on me, and now we can talk to each other. Something about that thing on your arm not knowing my language yet. They figured it out pretty quickly, though. And now I have this cool scar!" Paco turned his head and pointed. Yes, he had a scar. I didn't exactly think it looked cool, but it was there all right.

"Okay," I said. "So, what do I do now? Can we leave?" I turned to face the aliens.

The grays looked at me.

"No, you can't leave right now. Your planet is under attack by the orcs. The Council is intervening, but we think it's going to be awhile before you can head home." There was a long pause. "We think there's going to be a drastic change in your world coming out of this, but that'll be explained later. A lot of the policies have shifted with your world."

"Policies?"

"It's too much to get into right now. Let's just say your planet was quarantined, but now that you're here, you have some of the benefits the rest of the universe has. It was quickly passed by the Council after the orcs attacked and we started rescuing whoever we could."

Hello Chris. I am your designated AI. Today, you will be

picking your class. Your race has been auto-assigned to Human. Please pick your desired class from the list in front of you.

The voice came from the sleeve on my arm. As soon as it finished, an overlay appeared in my vision. I blinked, trying to understand what was going on. The overlay reminded me of a classic RPG game. Almost like *Bloodborne*. God, how I wanted to play the sequel right now. It was just a week out before I got into whatever *this* was. Now I feared it would be awhile before I could continue fighting in the Hunter's Dream.

Just play along. You'll wake up soon.

"How do I scroll through this list?" I asked.

Just think about it. It should come pretty quickly. If you want to examine a class further, just focus on it.

"I picked Fighter. Subclass, Samurai," Paco chimed in. I looked down at him with his little mask as he munched on a biscuit.

"Fighter? Samurai? Really? You?"

"I know the ways of the blade now. I will slay my foes with this stick." As soon as he said the words, a stick popped into existence. I focused on it.

Average Lackluster Stick.

It's nothing special. A piece of wood with a leaf growing off the side. Can be upgraded. Currently, it does not provide any stat buffs. But it makes a cool whooshing sound when you swing it at something.

"Pretty cool, huh?" Paco asked.

"Okay, so the talking raccoon wants to cut people in half. I guess I'll go with Ranger then." I made a quick choice.

The interface was more intuitive than I thought. I clicked on Ranger, and a slew of subclasses appeared in front of me. I'd played enough RPGs to know that if my friend here was going to be up close and personal with anything, I needed to stay back, but I absolutely hated any kind of spellcaster.

"Hunter subclass it is," I said as I clicked on the menu.

Congrats. You picked something entirely useless in space. Here's your bow, arrows, and a dagger. Remember to collect the arrows. You aren't special—yet. Maybe you never will be.

"Is the AI always like this?" I asked.

"Probably should have picked something cooler," the gray closest to me said.

Stat points have been auto-generated for newcomers. Chris, your stats are as follows:

Strength: 8

Dexterity: 8

Constitution: 6

Intelligence: 2

Wisdom: 4

Charisma: 1

"Really? Charisma is a 1? Intelligence a 2?"

You aren't as bright as you think you are, and your Charisma stems from your lackluster performance on the internet. People were more interested in Paco than they were in you. You were the insufferable host. Your guest was

the most interesting thing about you. Anyway, Paco's stats are as follows:

Strength: 8

Dexterity: 4

Constitution: 7

Intelligence: 3

Wisdom: 1

Charisma: 9

"How the fuck?"

"Don't question it, Chris. We both know I'm smarter. Also, my class choice gave me a better stat roll than you," Paco said. "Can I have a biscuit now?" he asked as he turned to the closest gray and rubbed his hands together.

"Anything for you, little guy," the gray smiled and walked to the opposite side of the room. He opened a drawer and came back with a green box.

"You know, Chris, mmm, these are great. You could learn a thing or two from these guys. Goddamn, yes. Anyway, yeah, Chris, your biscuits were good, but these things are otherworldly," Paco said between munches.

"Okay, okay. Enough of this. Why are we picking classes like we're in some kind of game?"

"Alright, this is a quick explanation," the gray who released me pulled up a chair. "You guys got ideas about RPGs because of how the universe actually works. Without the politics of it, humanity was barred from taking part in the actuality of it. Now that your planet is under attack, the Council has decided that whoever is not currently *on* the planet can choose to be a part of the greater universe. It's quite fun. You'll get lootboxes, kill bosses, and level up just like in the games you've played."

"Bosses? Like actual bosses?"

"Kinda. They're living things. If you kill them, they'll die a real death. And so will you. There's no respawning. Death is death."

"Quests? DO WE GET QUESTS? I *love* a good quest," Paco said as he finished his biscuit.

"What kind of quest have you ever gone on?" I asked.

"Thievery mostly. Sneaking around trying to get what I want. Bringing chaos to the world around me. Usual raccoon things. This one time, I went to the garbage dump. Man, I ate well that night. People throw so much out. Really wasteful, really. Besides, your quests are so *boring*. 'Oh, I went to the supermarket today. I grabbed a coffee to make myself *feel* better.' Have you ever watched the quests you guys go on day to day? Horrendous."

"And you nap all the time," I shot back at Paco.

"Good quests deserve a reward. A nap is a reward for a job well done."

I stood up and got off the table. My legs felt like jelly, and I also felt lighter. I was able to move more easily.

"Let me guess, gravity here isn't the same as on Earth?" I asked.

"It's about point eight percent of what you know. You'll get used to it. Just remember, whenever you go back, you'll have to readjust again."

I watched as Paco hopped off the table. I was still getting used to my new vision. There was a health bar in the top corner, and a blue one, which I assumed was my mana. A notification popped up. I quickly ignored it.

"Okay, give me a rundown. How do I access my bow, dagger, and arrows?"

Jesus fuck. Just think about it, and it'll pop up for you. Then drop shit into your hot bar like every game you've ever played. You don't pay attention to anything I say, do you? And you managed to pick a class all by yourself. Nothing ever clicks.

"Is he always this rude? Or is it just my AI?" I asked the gray in front of me.

"We have the same AI. He's really nice to me," Paco said, looking up at me.

Another notification popped up, and I once again waved it away.

I focused, and a dagger appeared in my hand. My arrows automatically equipped themselves on my back, along with my bow.

"Holy shit. Even if I am hallucinating, that's pretty cool."

My health bar dropped a bit, and I felt a sudden pain in my shin.

"Accept my party invite, you son-of-a—" Paco screeched.

"What the fuck!" I grabbed my shin and started rubbing the lump that had quickly formed.

There was a honking noise that erupted all around me like a flock of geese had arrived and surrounded me. I realized it was the grays. They were doubled over. They were *laughing*.

"I said, accept my party invite," Paco crossed closer to me wielding his stick. He was ready to swing it at me again.

I focused on the notifications I had been receiving and ignoring. They were all from Paco. I hit the checkmark next to his name.

Congratulations. You're now in a party. Maybe your new friend here will keep you from dying since you haven't accepted that this is real life and not just a hallucination like you continue to claim.

"Okay, there. We're in a party."

"Thank you, Chris." Paco chirped as he sat down and put his stick away.

"You could have just *said* something instead of hitting me."

"The AI told me you needed to get used to the interface, and it was better to just keep pinging you. I got mad when you ignored me."

PACO: and look, we can type. Secret message!

Chris: Great.

I sighed as the welt on my shin turned bright red.

"How do I get my health back?" I asked the grays and the AI. Whoever would listen honestly.

"Eating, drinking, sleeping, resting," one in the far corner responded. "You'll see once you inspect some food. Everything will have a description of what it does, just like your weapons, and Paco's stick." The gray was still wheezing the horrible goose sound.

"Okay. Is there anywhere for us to sleep on this ship?" I asked.

"Sure, let's show you your room. It's fully customizable. It's free while you're here, but once you leave to wherever you go, you'll need to purchase a house. Think of it like a safe room. All towns have them, and you'll see the door to yours with whatever you choose to decorate it with."

"That makes no sense, but okay."

"What doesn't make sense about it?" the gray turned back and asked.

"How will my house transfer to another town? It doesn't make sense."

"Oh, yeah, I guess that wouldn't make sense to you. You see, now that you're off your world and a part of the Council, there are some benefits you'll now enjoy. Think of it like walking into another dimension. The Council enacted this a long, long time ago. All of these towns have designated areas that allow visitors to return to their homes. But when they walk out the front door, it takes them to the last town they were in. Think of it like portal magic, but it's more like scientific wormhole knowledge. But yeah, just think of it like portal magic. Your small human brain understands that better."

"Small human brain, got it."

Paco and I followed the gray through a series of bulkhead doors that clinked and clanged when they opened and closed.

"This here will be your main entrance," the gray leading the way waved his arms at a door. It immediately turned into a tree and had a small hole in the middle.

"Sorry, I got excited," Paco said, staring up at me.

"You did that?" I asked.

"They said it was fully customizable."

"Well, how do *I* get in?" Just as I spoke, the door changed again. This time it had a handle, and a small round hole at the bottom which Paco quickly scurried through.

Inside there was a living room and a bathroom. There was a door for each of us on opposite sides of the room.

"This one's mine!" Paco shouted as he scampered to one of them. I watched it change from a large brown door into a manhole cover on the floor. Paco quickly lifted it and jumped in.

"Well, I guess I'll take this one," I muttered as I walked over to the brown door. "Okay, just focus."

I thought long and hard about the door. It changed to any color that came to my mind. I settled back on brown with a gold doorknob. It was easier and more intuitive than I had originally thought. Inside was my bedroom from Earth, just as I had left it. I smiled to myself. It was a nice comfort. The grays must have decorated this for me. I walked over to the bed and immediately passed out once my head hit the pillow.

CHAPTER 3

I WOKE to find myself in my room. There was murmuring coming from beyond the door. I quickly got up and opened it.

Shit. I'm still here.

Paco was talking to the grays who were in the living room.

They all turned to me.

"They have questions for you, Chris!"

"Uhhh, okay? Shoot."

"So…you guys worship the groundhog?"

"What?" I asked, perplexed.

"The groundhog! You know, the one you guys celebrate every year," Paco shouted.

"I mean, kinda? Most of us hate him because he goes back to sleep. I wouldn't say we worship—"

"And he can see into the future?" one of them asked pointedly. I watched them all lean forward.

I had to think about the question. "I mean, I guess? Technically? I don't think that's how it works."

"What a wondrous line of evolution. He's a god!" One of the grays got overly excited and started muttering to the others on the red leather couch, which I assumed was Paco's idea.

"No, he's a rat that just goes to sleep."

"Hey, I take offense to that," Paco shot at me. He squinted his eyes.

"You are not a rat, Paco."

"It is still a slur for my people. Besides, rats aren't *nearly* as smart as I am."

"That's kinda cheating. These guys here made you smarter with that implant," I gestured towards them.

"I am the king of raccoons, and all will bow at my feet." Paco stood up, then jumped on the coffee table and held his stick high in the air.

"Look what you guys did. Now I have to deal with this sass all the time," I said.

The grays whispered to each other a moment before one spoke.

"We've been discussing this in private. Paco can stay with us if he chooses. And you can go on your way."

"I can't abandon my squire," Paco said as he lowered his stick and faced the grays.

"I'm not your—"

Before I could finish my sentence, the name next to my health bar changed. **Chris, Squire of King Paco: First of His Name, Leader of the Free World.**

I sighed and checked my party menu. Sure enough, there it was. Paco's name had unnecessary identifiers after it.

"Don't worry, I'll still let you call me Paco as long as you get me biscuits whenever I want," he said as he hopped off the table and came to beg at my feet.

"Is this my actual name now?" I asked the AI.

Technically, no. It's just an identifier for your party. Paco doesn't hold any royal titles—yet. He'll appear as Paco to anyone you meet, and you'll still appear as Chris, unfortunately. If and when Paco gets a royal title, then the real fun begins.

"So, if *I* get a royal title, something cool happens?" I asked.

Won't happen. Useless. Total waste of meat. That's you.

I listened to the AI cackle. Something told me it didn't actually hate me; it just enjoyed being a complete dick. I kept my mouth shut as I sat on the couch.

Anyway, back to business. You both leveled up. You'll get some lootboxes for forming a party and gaining your first level. Sit down and see what you guys got.

Paco jumped up next to me on the couch while the grays watched us. I let Paco go first as he pulled out his first box.

Wooden Beginner Box.

I watched as he opened it, and a bunch of leaves dumped themselves onto the floor, then disappeared as quickly as they had manifested themselves. I inspected the item as soon as Paco began holding it.

It's a string. Attach it to your stick and wrap it around your cute little wrist. Now you can throw your stick and

drag it back to you. This item provides no buffs.It can be cut, but there may be a few upgrades in your future that may make it virtually indestructible.

"I can throw the stick!" Paco screamed as he equipped the string. It looped around his wrist and the bottom of his stick. Sure enough, he threw it across the room, and it made a whooshing noise before it clacked to the floor. He pulled it back.

"I also got some health potions, and a mana potion," he said. "What'd you get?" he asked as he looked over to me. His tail jerked back and forth with anticipation.

"I got three boxes."

"Three? That's not fair." Paco's tail lowered, and he crossed his arms as he leaned back into the couch.

Useless Waste of Meat Box.

I sighed and opened it. The box disappeared, and raw chicken fell into my lap with a squelching sound.

Raw Chicken.

You *can* eat it, but you will probably get sick. Cook this bad boy up, and maybe you'll make something good out of it. Provides no buffs, just sickness. Cooking may provide buffs. Honestly, it'll probably just restore some health, but who cares? Congrats on the chicken!

I opened my next box. It was also a **Wooden Beginner Box**. It only had health potions and a single mana potion.

"Guess you got the lucky one with the item," I turned to Paco.

"Yeah, but your class came with three weapons; I only got one. It's only fair."

I chuckled. Paco was more and more annoyed by the single box.

"Woah," I said as Paco and the grays looked at the last box. Its golden color was covered in blue and green gemstones.

Golden Box of the Squire.

"I feel like these aren't the actual names and the AI is just fucking with me," I said with disdain.

Nope. Totally the names. I would never.

I ignored the commentary and opened the box. Rainbows and fanfare erupted out of it. I pulled out a single vial.

Potion. One time use.

There was scribbling after which I couldn't understand. It was a mix of circles, triangles, squares, and shapes I didn't have names for.

You will not be able to read this description until prerequisites have been met. Like it says, onetime use. You will know.

"Uhhh, okay." I tucked the vial into my inventory. Next to it, there were ten money signs. "I guess it's worth a lot."

"How many dollar signs?" one of the grays asked.

"Ten."

They all gasped and looked back at each other.

"That's enough to buy your own spaceship. Make sure you keep it safe. You should probably give it to Paco."

I looked over at him. He rubbed his hands together, just waiting for me to concede the potion to him.

"I'll keep it," I said.

Well, okay then. Paco, since your party member is so *selfish*, I've decided to give you something myself.

"Yes!"

A hamster appeared on the coffee table. It didn't move.

Hamster of Holding. It's like a Bag of Holding, but it's cute. Items will be stored in its cheeks and stomach. Sometimes they come out a little slimy. Doubles inventory capacity. No, he doesn't speak. No, he's not a pet. He's a hamster that holds things.

"Gross…"

"I *love* it," Paco shouted as he picked up the hamster and equipped it. The hamster hung on a string that looped around Paco's waist.

Sorry. It was the best I could do. No one really likes the Hamster of Holding, so they're generally free to anyone who wants one.

"Can I get one?" I asked. I didn't really *want* one. But carrying more things would be nice.

No, you're selfish.

"That's fine," I muttered. "So, how do we level up more?" I asked as I turned to the grays and leaned forward. They were still oooing and ahhing at Paco's new string and hamster.

"We can take you to one of our hunting grounds. There's a planet a galaxy or two over that is home to some dwarves and dragons. Don't worry, they keep the peace between each other," one of them said.

"Like, *real* dragons?" Paco asked.

"Correct, little one. Dragons that shoot fire, sleep on gold, and fly around. They're not very nice to visitors. That's why we'll take you to the dwarven home. They accept foreigners. You can farm some XP and get some gold."

"Sounds like a good plan," I said. "Will any of you be joining us?"

"Oh, absolutely not. Too dangerous. We'll drop you in a low-level area, and you'll fight some rats, snakes, rabbits. Maybe cut down a tree or two. Work on just getting your level up. We prefer to stay on the ship rather than fight in hand-to-hand combat."

"Uh, okay. Also, what're your names? The AI hasn't told me anything."

"I'm Curly. This is John, and that one is Ralph."

"'Curly'… got it."

"Yes, it's because I'm bald," Curly replied. "Anyway, make yourselves comfortable and *do not eat*. Once we jump to the next galaxy, you'll probably be sick, and our little robots don't like cleaning up puke."

I looked over at Paco. "No more biscuits, 'little one,'" I smiled.

Paco flipped me off in return and walked over to the manhole cover. He quickly moved it and slammed it shut. I laughed.

"You guys made him upset," I said to the grays in front of me.

They shrugged in return. "Better for him to be mad than sick. Poor guy, though. Just wants his biscuits."

I sat down on the couch and waited as the grays disappeared.

"What the fuck did I get myself into?"

CHAPTER 4

HA! **Idiot. You're nauseous. Congrats on the debuff. It'll go away in five minutes, but it's fun watching you suffer a bit.**

I stood up, and my equilibrium was definitely off. I tried to walk forward, but found myself leaning to one side and then the other, like I was back on a cruise ship. I put my hand out and placed it on the coffee table as I tried to steady myself.

"Nauseous isn't the right word. I feel like I'm borderline blackout drunk." I attempted to focus my vision. There was a timer steadily ticking down from five minutes. "Okay, it'll be over soon," I said as I closed my eyes and took deep breaths.

"Chris, I don't feel so good," Paco's voice came from behind me. It grated on my ears. It was like a child screaming in a restaurant. In that moment, I hated him.

"It's alright; we'll be okay in a few minutes," I replied. I heard a gagging sound. It only annoyed me more.

"Chris, I frew up," he whined. "It's all over me and my room."

"It's okay; the robots will clean it. We'll get you in the shower once the debuff goes away," I waved my hand towards him as I tried to balance myself and breathe.

"No, Curly's gonna be so mad at me. He told me not to eat, and I didn't listen. Chris, they're gonna be so mad. I don't want them to be mad at me," he whined.

"Jesus Christ, it's fine. There's thirty seconds left," I started counting to myself.

The debuff went away, and I immediately felt better. I looked over to Paco, who was standing there covered in chunky brown vomit. I laughed.

"It's not *funny!*"

"You didn't just eat a biscuit; you ate a lot of them."

"I'm going to wash myself off," he shouted as he ran for the bathroom. I heard the water start running.

Curly, Ralph, and John came in, but I couldn't tell which was which. I had names, but they had no identifiable features. I waited for one to speak.

"How are you feeling?" Curly asked. Finally, their names appeared above them.

"I feel okay now," I said. "Paco threw up a bit in his room. He's cleaning himself off right now."

Curly sighed and turned away. "I'll let the robots know," he said as he stepped out.

Paco came out of the bathroom. His eyes were wide, and he looked like he was about to cry at a moment's notice.

"I'm sorry," he muttered. "I didn't listen. And your

biscuits are just so much better than that *garbage* Chris gives me."

"Hey!"

"I'm sorry, but it's true. You humans could learn a thing or two from these guys about appropriate snacks. It's about *balance* and *flavor*. Not just sugar and additives."

I rolled my eyes as Curly returned with a robot in tow. He whispered and pointed to the manhole cover on the floor. The robot looked dejected, as if it had taken a big sigh when it looked down at the floor. It wheeled itself over, lifted the manhole with a little arm, and hopped down.

There were mixed electrical sounds that erupted from beneath our feet. I thought for a moment that the robot had short-circuited.

"Oh, he made a real big mess down there," Curly said.

"I didn't mean it!" Paco shouted back.

"It's okay, little one," Curly said as he crossed over and knelt down beside Paco. He rubbed his head. "Are you ready to go on an adventure? You get to use your stick now."

Paco's eyes lit up. He started scampering in circles around the living room.

"Okay, but how are we going to get to the planet? Land on it, or are you going to teleport us like they do in *Star Trek?*"

"Please, that would waste way too much energy. We're going to land at their starport. We'll stay there a bit, and you guys can explore the town. Then we're going to leave awhile to discuss with the Council what is happening with the orcs."

"Okay. Come on, Paco. Let's go watch these guys land a spaceship."

We walked out the door and went through another series of bulkheads until we arrived at the cockpit. It was massive, at least five times larger than the room where they had strapped me down to the table. The walls were lined with seats, and glass surrounded the entirety of it. Curly stood at the command console in the center of the room while John and Ralph each took a seat on either side of him. There were more grays in here with us, but none of them introduced themselves or had names above their heads.

"Begin our descent. Increase thrust," he said.

The grays on either side started clicking away at the screens in front of them in unison. It was like watching an opera live. Curly was the conductor, and the other two were the musicians. It truly was a sight to see. The ship lurched forward, and I had to plant myself firmly on the ground. A steering wheel appeared. Curly grabbed it, then pushed it forward.

"Just like taking the subway," I said to no one in particular.

I watched through the glass as we began our descent onto the planet. A wave of blue shimmered as we closed in, then a wave of fire appeared in front of the ship.

"What's that?" I pointed and asked Curly.

"Shields, of course."

"I kinda figured, but thought I'd ask." I turned to look back at the planet coming into view as we breached the atmosphere.

"Small human brain," I heard him whisper.

I watched as continents and oceans started to appear more

recognizable. Mountains covered in snow littered the landscape, and in the far off distance, I could see a continent covered in soot as black smoke rose from a monstrous volcano which spewed lava down its sides.

"Look! That must be where the dragons live!" Paco pointed to what I was already looking at. His eyes were wide as he beamed with excitement.

"Where are we landing?" I asked.

Curly pointed to my left. I could see a beautiful forest. The trees had a mixture of pink and green leaves. They were huge, like redwoods, but not all clustered together. Each tree was about a football field away from the next, at least, I guessed.

The ship stopped its descent abruptly, and I felt like I was on the subway again. I braced myself against the console to stop myself from falling over. Paco wasn't as lucky. He launched over the front and crashed to the floor.

"You okay, little one?" Curly looked over the console.

Paco lifted his hand . "Yeah, if I had opposable thumbs, I'd give you a thumbs up." He stood up and scratched the back of his head.

"Good. We're changing course to the starport."

The ship lurched, but not nearly as harshly as before. I watched as we coasted through the sky. We buried ourselves in the clouds, and when we reemerged, I could see small towns coming into view. Little wooden cabins dotted the landscape between the green and pink leaves.

"You know, when you said dwarves, I figured they lived in the mountains."

"Oh, they do. That's where they do most of their work, but they live in the sunlight. Common misconception, but you get the point. They take pride in their work."

I saw the starport as we got closer. There was a wooden tower with a layered stone roof. It wasn't much different from an air traffic control tower.

"Yer cleared to land," a gruff voice burst through the comms above our heads.

Curly nodded to his co-pilots.

There was an open field at the starport, and the ship landed softly. No jarring crash, no noise as it lowered itself into the space it was designated for. No whining of engines, just a simple descent, which felt like parking an electric car. Paco and I followed the grays through the bulkhead doors and into an airlock. There was a quick hiss as white steam coated us.

"Just a decontaminant. Eliminates any viruses or bacteria you may have. Can't have you killing a bunch of foreigners again with the germs you carry," Curly smiled at me.

I nodded.

We stepped out of the airlock. There was a set of stairs. Above, the sun shone brightly. It was nice feeling the sun on my skin again. Something almost comforting. There was a dwarf waiting for us at the bottom of the staircase.

"Ay, nice to see ya'll again. And you two must be the visitors from Earth." He extended his hand. I shook it. His skin was calloused, hard, and I thought he might break my hand in the vice-grip.

"I'm Chris, and this is Paco."

"I'm Brukrag Oakshoulder. But you can call me Bruk."

Achievement Unlocked.

Visit a foreign planet. And not get killed immediately! Congrats. Though I would have loved to see a shower of blood and gore the second you got here. Oh well, beggars can't be choosers. Enjoy your boxes.

"Come, come," Bruk waved us on to follow him. "Ya'll can open your boxes inside. There's a storm a comin'."

I looked up and didn't see any foreboding clouds. "Really? It doesn't look like it."

"Yeh, about an hour out. Needle rain. Pesky thing."

Paco looked up at me. "Chris, what is 'needle rain'?"

I shrugged and followed Bruk into the main building of the starport. Inside there were dwarves everywhere. All of them were about four feet tall and stocky, like offensive linemen, but not chunky. They were all hiding abs under their clothes. They reminded me of the Amish in the way they dressed. Very kind. They all waved to us as we passed.

"Are we the first visitors from Earth?"

"Ay, first Terrans to ever make it to our home. You're basically mini-celebrities. It's an honor. I hope the orcs are stopped soon, then we can really share our cultures."

I wanted to ask what they knew about the attack on Earth, but at that very moment, I didn't. Hopefully, my friends and family were still alive, or saved by another ship. Anything. I didn't want to think of what the orcs could possibly be doing to destroy Earth, or why they were doing it.

We sat down at a large wooden table. It was sturdy, but

shorter than I would have liked. My knees were almost touching the bottom of it when I sat down in the small chair.

"Open yer boxes, then we can start gettin' ye' leveled."

Silver Beginner Box.

I opened it. There was no fanfare this time. Inside was a pair of boots.

Leather Boots of the Ranger.

They're not the prettiest, or the most manly. Kinda plain, honestly. But they get the job done. You can move stealthily wearing these bad boys.

Wearer now makes no noise when walking through brush. Leaves don't crunch under your feet. Sticks if broken still make a sound, but it's not nearly as harsh as it would be. You can still draw attention, but most people, animals, or things that hear it probably will just brush it off. Except ghosts, wisps, and other-worldly beings. They'll probably come. Fast.

"Neat. This is actually pretty cool," I said as I took off my shoes, placed them in my inventory, and pulled on the leather boots. They resized themselves to fit my feet, which piqued my interest. It felt like I was wearing almost nothing, like I was barefoot with how well they fit.

"Okay, now me!" Paco screeched. He hopped down from his chair and produced his own lootbox.

Golden Beginner Box. Free upgrade from Silver since your party member is selfish.

I sighed.

Paco opened his box, and fireworks erupted from it like on the Fourth of July. He stared in amazement.

Red and Yellow Vehicle.

It's definitely a knock-off of those children's cars everyone either had or used growing up. If you can think it, it can do it! This vehicle has telepathic capabilities. Change the color? Think it. Want it to fly? Too bad there are limitations, but it can hover and hop. Maybe even glide across the water for a bit, but don't get too crazy; you'll probably sink, eventually. And please, *for the love of God, don't think it'll blow up because this bad boy will most definitely explode.* **Like I said, there are limitations, but that is something it will one hundred percent do if you think about it.**

"This. Is. Awesome! Chris, watch this!"

I watched as the red and yellow children's toy turned jet-black. The front turned into one of those plates that old trains had. Then spikes grew out of it. I watched as Paco kept thinking of anything he could. An engine block appeared in the back of it, like one from a drag car. Black smoke billowed out of the exhaust pipes on either side of it. Everyone cheered and laughed. I looked around at everyone celebrating him and smiled to myself.

I turned back and examined the new vehicle again.

Paco's War Wagon.

"Oh, fuck off," I laughed.

I watched Paco get into his war wagon and race around the starport. He twisted and turned the steering wheel, driving in circles. More than once he almost flipped over as he drifted the ass-end of that little toy. It was nice to get my mind off the events of the last two days. All I could think about for that moment was how fast that little car went. He pulled up next to me.

"Get in," he said as he reached over and pushed open the door.

"I can't. The roof is in the way." I watched as the car changed shape again. The seat raised higher, and part of the roof disappeared so I could sit comfortably. I pulled myself in. A seatbelt magically appeared and buckled itself. Paco took off for the exit.

CHAPTER 5

"DON'T you think we should have asked Bruk where the town is?" I shouted over the roar of the engine. Paco had grown more confident in his driving. The war wagon ripped down the dirt road, spewing black smoke in its wake. I thought we were gaining speed, which only meant that Paco wished for the car to go faster.

"I think Mr. Shoulder will be okay with a little fun right now," he said as he took a corner way too hard. We skidded off the road and into a ditch. Thank God I was buckled in;, otherwise, I would have gotten thrown into a tree.

"My wagon!" Paco shouted as he hopped out to assess the damage.

"It doesn't look so bad. Maybe you should think of a way for this thing to get more traction, and also a roll cage so if we flip it we don't, you know, die."

The passenger door was completely smashed in, and the

roof had been completely torn off. One of the wheels was bent sideways. It could have been worse, honestly.

Paco walked closer to the war wagon and pulled it into his inventory. "Let's walk for now," he said. "Maybe we can find some stuff to kill on our way to town."

"We don't even know where it is."

"Didn't you see the signs while we were driving? It's four miles west." Paco pointed down the road he had tried to turn onto.

"No, I was holding on for dear life."

"Whatever. Let's go, Chris." Paco scampered off into the woods instead of following the road.

"I don't think we should go this way," I said.

"I doubt there's going to be much this close to the road for us to worry about. Plus, it'll let you get used to hunting with a bow." Paco started to climb a tree. When he got to one of the larger branches, he equipped his stick as he took the pose of a fencer. He started to swing and stab the air around him. Each time he did, the stick made its classic whooshing sound. I equipped my bow and pulled out one of my arrows. I rested it against the string and walked forward.

"You know, this feels pretty natural to me," I said. "Almost like I've done this before."

"I think it's because of our classes. We have basic instincts of how we're supposed to attack."

You are correct, little one. You both have basics that help your class. You'll have to level up your abilities. Now that you're no longer in a safe area, you can see what those abilities are in your hotbar.

I looked and saw a few. **Hunter's Instinct**. It marked targets within fifty feet of me. **Deadeye**. That one increased damage two and a half times if I shot something in the head. And I had a magic ability. **Heal.** It cost five mana to cast, but raised my health by fifty percent.

"What'd you get?" I asked after telling Paco what I had.

"I also got **Heal.** Then there's **Double Slash**. It hits a target twice for each swing. There's a cooldown on it for a few minutes. If I use a sword it has a fifty percent chance to inflict **Bleed.** Right now it has a five percent chance to inflict **Stun** because I'm using the stick. Then I have **Second Wind** which grants me ten percent of my life back. That has a ten hour long cooldown."

Use that one sparingly. It doesn't require mana like Heal does, so you can use it after the cooldown, but it should be used when you *desperately* need it. Don't need you relying on it and then not being able to use it when you *really* need it.

Paco climbed down the tree and came to my side. We walked further west.

"Shoot it, Chris," Paco whispered.

Ahead of us, there was a large bird. It was a **level 5 demon hawk**. Its wings were obsidian. Its torso was white, and it had bright red eyes.

"Okay, just be quiet and stay here," I whispered as I skulked forward. I tried not to step on any twigs, even though my boots would deaden most of the noise. I didn't know anything about this thing, and I didn't really want to find out. It was only three levels higher than us, but I wasn't comfortable actually killing something. I pulled myself next to a tree and slammed down on my **Deadeye** as I leveled my bow and knocked an arrow. I loosed it. The arrow pierced straight through the demon hawk's eye with a sickening squelch. It went out the other side and slammed into a tree. The bird flopped over without knowing what hit it.

"You did it!" Paco yelled from behind. I heard him running through the brush. He pounced and hit me directly between the shoulders, almost knocking me over. He had tried to use me as a springboard. He rocketed towards the dead demon hawk. I ran over, but it had already been looted.

"Nothing really here," he said.

"That was my loot because it was my kill," I said as I put my bow on my back.

"You really are selfish. You got most of the XP for the kill, and now you won't share the loot? Fine, take it." Paco produced **demon hawk breasts**. They plopped onto the ground in a pile. "Here, take the feathers, too." He handed those to me. They were a mix of white and black. The white ones were shorter than the black ones, which had obviously come from the wings of the bird.

"What else was there?" I asked.

"I'm keeping the skull," he retorted.

"Skull?"

"Yeah, it says you can wear it." Paco put the skull on. It formed over his head and resized itself just like my boots had. The beak elongated in front of his face. He truly was something to see: a raccoon wearing a hawk skull.

"I hate it. I can't see anything," he said as he took it off and stowed it in his Hamster of Holding. I watched as it opened its mouth and swallowed the skull. It had enlarged itself, then shrunk down to its original size. The whole scene was off-putting, to say the least.

My XP bar had gone up halfway from killing the hawk. Paco's went up about a quarter. It wasn't much, but if we kept killing low-level enemies, surely we'd hit level three by the time we made it to town.

We heard a screech that sounded like nails against a chalkboard mixed with metal scraping against metal. Paco's tail shot straight up, and his eyes grew wide as the hair on my arms stood at attention. We both turned our heads and saw it.

Level 15 demon hawk.

This is the mother of the demon hawk you just killed. Poor baby. He was just venturing outside of the nest for the first time, and Chris decided it would be a good idea to put an arrow right through its soft, squishy eyeball like it was a juicy grape. Now, Mama is mad. Like, really mad. Enraged even. Who would have thought that killing her son would make her this mad? I certainly didn't see it coming. Not in a million years. Anyway, she's coming for you. Luckily, dad hasn't heard the news yet. You'd be all around fucked if he wasn't at work.

"Run!" I shouted to Paco.

The demon hawk was massive. Easily the size of a black bear. Her color was the same except for a few red feathers that sat atop her head. She screeched again before she opened her wings to take flight towards us.

Even with my new boots, I heard the leaves crunch and

twigs break as he ran towards town. We aimed for a denser section of trees, hoping it would stop the demon hawk from gaining on us.

Paco looked up at the sky and saw her soaring overhead. He pointed at her. It was like a goddamn police helicopter circling, waiting for the criminal to come back into view.

"What's the plan, Chris?" Paco asked, panting as we started to slow.

"We have to get to town; we'll be safe there at least."

"How do you know that?"

"In all the games I played, the town is almost always safe."

"This isn't a game, Chris!"

"I know, but maybe the dwarves can help us."

"Mr. Shoulder is going to be pissed at you. Not at me. But definitely at you," Paco said.

I rubbed my hands against my face. I just wanted to be home.

"Let's go." I turned and started going through the denser forest towards town.

The demon hawk continued to screech overhead as we made slow progress. I was grateful that the leaves of the canopy were thick, even though it made this section of forest more miserable to get through.

As the forest grew less dense, we could see the fortifications at the edge of town, maybe a quarter mile away. A massive wall of wood stood surrounding the area. Each log was sharpened into a point. We waited just at the edge of the woods.

"Hold on," Paco said before he turned and ran back the way we came.

"What the hell is he doing?"

Hunting.

The AI on my arm decided to chime in.

"For what?"

Paco re-emerged from the denser section holding a snake.

Level 2 snake. Nothing special. Poisonous. Don't get bitten.

This was the shortest description I'd seen in a while. Then I noticed Paco was now at level 3.

"Congrats," I said.

"Thanks, I'm gonna keep the teeth."

"How'd you know it was back there?"

"I saw it when we were running, but I was more worried about staying alive than whacking it with my stick." He threw it on the ground in front of me. Sure enough, it had no teeth. "Keep the meat if you want."

I inspected it and stuffed a single **snake cutlet** into my inventory.

"Okay, how do we get to town without that thing killing us?" Paco asked as he came and stood next to me at the edge of the forest staring towards the town.

"Take out your war wagon and see if it runs. That's our best bet."

Paco's War Wagon dropped in front of us. It was still spewing black smoke, and the engine still ran. Paco hopped into it and revved the engine.

"I think it works," Paco said as he tried to adjust the

rearview mirror, which magically appeared. He imagined that the rear tire was fixed.

I hopped in and nodded to Paco. He floored it so hard that my head hit a piece of the roof as I was thrown back into my seat. This time I didn't buckle in. I needed a clear view when Mama Bird came screeching for her revenge.

"Give it more power," I shouted as I produced my bow. I stood up, trying to balance myself and my bow.

The demon hawk was now in full view. She soared above the trees and dove behind us. She was lining up for the kill. I watched as her feet turned to a chrome color, and her talons elongated at least three feet. She had definitely cast some kind of spell or ability. I knew that if she caught up, we were most certainly dead.

"I'm trying! But it's fighting me! It doesn't want to go any faster!"

"Shit," I said. I knocked one of my precious arrows and let it fly at the hawk. I missed entirely. I pulled another and let it go, still missing.

"We're almost there!" Paco shouted.

"Third time's the charm," I whispered as I tried to calm my breathing. I let the arrow go. It soared and found its mark. The demon hawk screamed bloody murder. A health bar appeared above it. It had barely gone down. But it did what I needed it to. She veered off and circled back.

The gates to the town opened, and Paco slammed on the brakes. I watched the world spin as I was tossed through the open section of the war wagon.

CHAPTER 6

MY HEAD WAS POUNDING. I sat up. Vertigo had kicked in. Buildings spun, and shapes of dwarves came running to my side as I tried to get a bearing on my surroundings. I looked at my inventory. My health was red. I slammed my **Heal** spell and watched my health climb back up. It took a moment to register, but the obvious concussion slowly faded.

Paco came bounding over to me and plopped down. His tail twitched as he did. He looked scared, but also excited from the rush of adrenaline coursing through his body.

"They killed the mama bird once we got inside. Ballistas appeared out of those two roofs," he pointed at a pair of buildings. There were no ballistas on top of them.

"Where'd the ballistas go?"

"I don't know. There was a crunching sound, and they slowly descended. I guess they're on like an elevator."

"Interesting," I said, looking down at the raccoon. He was twiddling his fingers. "What's wrong?"

"They wouldn't let me keep its talons. I wanted them."

"Well, it wasn't your kill. You can't go stealing everything just because you want it."

Paco looked up at me in annoyance. "I know," he muttered. "But I still want them."

"Maybe we can level up and get you some talons later."

"Like a quest?!"

"Yes, like a quest."

New Quest!

This is a party quest. Get Paco the talons of a demon hawk. A mother or a father will do. Baby demon hawks will not drop talons as loot. Do they have magical properties? Who knows! There's only one way to find out.

Reward: nothing. You get talons that you have to give Paco.

"Chris, our first *real* quest," his eyes lit up.

"Yeah, I got the same thing," I said, scrolling through my menu. I pushed myself up off the ground now that the world had finally stopped spinning. Paco walked on all fours. It was strange to me. He could obviously run on both legs with whatever the grays did to him, but he still chose to walk around like the raccoon I knew him as.

There were dwarves throughout the town. The women dressed like old-timey fantasy women with white blouses and brown dresses that had overall straps going over the shoulders. Most of the men were clad in leather and animal pelts. There were foxes, coyotes, and the occasional albino animal skin draped over their shoulders as we walked further into town. I opened my map and could see the center filled with merchants.

"Let's go here," I pointed to the map. A red ping placed itself. I put my map away and saw that the marker had generated itself into the world. There was a glowing beam that reached to the sky in front of us.

"Chris, do you think other people can see that?"

Before I could speak, the AI chimed in.

No. This is a marker designated only to the party. Unless, of course, someone has a spell that allows them to see markers by other people. Then, that would be bad. Highly unlikely here, but still, keep that in mind, little one.

"Understood," I said.

The center of town was bustling with people laughing, playing music on instruments I didn't understand, and dancing. Merchants argued back and forth with customers and sold their wares.

"By the gods!" a familiar voice shouted.

"Mr. Shoulder!" Paco shouted as he ran up to the dwarf.

"We thought you were dead once you took off in your war wagon."

"Good to see you, Bruk," I said as I nodded my head.

"By the ax of Lord Greatwood, may our swords never dull and our shields never splinter. With his fury, may the ground we walk upon give way to dust and rubble. With his patience, may the waves still and the winds fall silent in our presence. With his mercy, may our souls find peace within the earth we once emerged. Lord Greatwood, guide my hand. I am Brukrag, your humble vassal, come to this land to do thy bidding until I am once again called home. Hoy."

"What?" I asked.

"It's just a prayer in my culture."

"Who's Lord Greatwood?" Paco asked.

"Not now, little one. I'll tell you at our feast later." Oakshoulder reached town and patted Paco on the head.

"Feast?"

"Of course! Always a feast when we have guests." He laughed a hearty laugh. "Let me show you the guest quarters. Come." Brukrag turned away and started walking away from the center.

The buildings became less ornate as we walked a couple of blocks. The wood carvings slowly disappeared, and all that remained were wooden buildings shaped like blocks.

"Pick any of 'em, they'll take you to your rooms." Brukrag waved his arm at a row of buildings. All brown. All brown doors. All with handles made of wood.

"Where should we meet you later for the feast, Mr. Shoulder?"

"Pull up your map."

Paco scrolled through his menu and got to his map. I watched as Brukrag touched the empty air in front of him. There was a blue marker that appeared.

"How'd you do that?"

"I'm the mayor of this town. I have abilities to do things most can't. You'll find other mayors can do this as well," he said. "Anyway, go there when the sun begins to set. It's time for me to go. By the ax of Lord Greatwood, may our swords never dull and our shields never splinter. With his fury, may the ground we walk upon give way to dust and rubble. With his patience, may the waves still and the winds fall silent in our presence. With his mercy, may our souls find peace within the earth we once emerged. Lord Greatwood, guide my hand. I am Brukrag, your humble vassal, come to this land to do thy bidding until I am once again called home. Hoy." He nodded and turned away before Paco or I could say anything.

I found it annoying that he repeated the same prayer.

"Okay, so which one?" Paco asked, snapping me out of my inner thoughts.

"Any of them. Just go to that door," I pointed at the closest building.

I put my hand on the wooden handle, depressed it, and opened the door. Inside was our common room, just as we had left it.

Paco's eyes widened. "That's crazy," he whispered before he trotted off and pulled the manhole cover to his room. I watched his feet and tail slide away.

CHAPTER 7

"HEY, CHRIS," Paco lifted the manhole cover to his room and peeked out. "Do you

wanna go explore the town a bit before the feast?"

"Yeah, we should probably get our bearings a bit."

I had been sitting on the couch scrolling through my menus and hot listing items I thought would be beneficial. It was mainly a way for me to get used to pulling them up in case of a fight. I specifically set that secret potion as the last option, should it ever tell me what it did. I wasn't holding my breath based on the description.

Paco and I went out in search of any businesses. We didn't have any gold, but at least we could get the lay of the land once we started leveling up and coming back here.

"What's that?" he pointed at a building with a black anvil engraved on the side.

"A blacksmith. They make armor and swords. It looks like

the one with the books is probably spells. The bottle is potions." I started listing off things without truly knowing, but having played enough games in my life, I assumed I was correct.

"What about the bed?"

"Maybe an Inn?"

"Why do they need an inn if they have an entire section for visitors?"

"Good question. Wanna check it out?"

I didn't get an answer. Paco ran towards the door and opened it.

Inside, there was a female dwarf behind the bar. She was surrounded by taps for beer. There was a pleasant aroma coming from somewhere. It was a mixture of beef, thyme, and oregano. Paco was already at the bar talking her ear off.

"Chris! This is Wilduwen Maplefinger. She's really nice."

"Oh, stop, sweetie. I'm plenty mean to the regulars here. You guys caused quite the commotion already. We all thought our new visitors had been killed before we had gotten the chance to get to know you two. That would have been a sad time."

"Yeah, and then we met back up with Mr. Shoulder, and he's gonna have a feast for us tonight."

"Mr. Shoulder?" she asked.

"Brukrag Oakshoulder," I interjected.

"Oh! The mayor. A fine gentleman and a great leader. He fought an entire army of goblins in his younger years with his wolf, Dimitry. Poor thing."

"What happened?" Paco asked.

"Dimitry, unfortunately, succumbed to his wounds. He carries him around wherever he goes now."

"Is that the white cloak he wears?"

"That is correct, sweetie. It's a great honor for a man to personally skin and tan the hide of his warbeast. It's a reminder of the bond they once shared. May they meet again at the gates of Valhalla," she bowed her head.

Paco looked over at me, and I knew what was coming. "Would you skin and tan me if I died in a great battle with you?"

"Can I turn you into a hat?" I asked.

"That's not funny. I'd rather be a satchel. At least then I'm useful. Or turn me into something cool, like a pair of moccasins."

Wilduwen laughed. "You two bickering is really cute."

I watched Paco smile and continue asking the bartender questions. I walked around admiring the place. It reminded me of an old Western diner. Everything was made out of wood, but the floors looked to be freshly polished. There was not a single mark anywhere to be seen. I walked back over to the bar and plopped myself down next to Paco.

"Anything for you?" Wilduwen asked.

"No thanks, I don't have any money. Neither does Paco."

"Foolish. You're great guests in our town. I insist. We have light and dark ale."

"I'll take the light one!" Paco shouted.

"I guess I'll try the dark."

Wilduwen stepped away and brought us back two pints.

Paco quickly picked his up and started gulping it down. He coughed half of it back into the glass.

"This is gross!"

"Paco! Shut up," I said.

"It's quite okay. It takes a few to get used to the taste. Just sip it and you'll love it," Wilduwen said.

I took a sip from mine. The amber-colored alcohol tasted like cherries and coffee with chocolate mixed in. It immediately went to my head.

"This is great, but I already feel drunk."

"Yeah, the way we make it gets into your bloodstream faster," Wilduwen laughed. "I'll bring you guys some water."

I turned toward Paco, who was casually trying to sip his without making a face.

"Chris, who's that guy behind you staring?"

I turned and saw the man Paco was talking about. He looked like Aragorn from the *Lord of the Rings* movies when he sat alone at the pub. He had a black cloak pulled up covering his face, but I could see the glinting of eyes beneath the darkness of his hood.

"Excuse me, Wilduwen," I said when she came back with our waters. "Who's the guy in the corner?" I gave a slight tilt of my head as she looked over to him.

"I, uh, I think you should quit drinking and go over to talk to him," she said with wide eyes. She took our glasses away and walked to the back of the Inn.

I looked at Paco, who was growing more nervous by the moment. I watched him rub his hands together and look every which way he could as he purposely tried to avoid eye contact with the cloaked man.

"Come on," I said as I pushed myself away from the bar.

Paco: Chris, I don't want to

Chris: I don't either. He's making the hair on my arms stand up, but Wilduwen said we should.

Paco: Okay, but you go first, so if anything happens, I'll go get Mr. Shoulder

I sighed and walked over to the table. I grabbed the chair directly opposite the man. Paco stood next to me, never sitting down.

"Hello, friendsss," the man hissed.

"Hello," I said shortly.

"What bringsss you here?"

I looked at Paco, who had his shoulders hunched as he continued to rub his paws together.

"We saw you looking at us. We were wondering who you were and just wanted to introduce ourselves. I'm Chris, and this is Paco."

"I'm Sssly, your friendly neighborhood merchant. Pleassse step inssside." I watched the cloaked man wave his hand to the side. A door appeared on the wall. It was wide open, but I could not see anything but total darkness.

Paco: Chris we shouldn't

I looked around. There was no one else in the place with us.

Chris: I don't think we have much of a choice in the matter.

I walked up to the empty void and felt it pulling me in. Then the world went black.

———

I was sitting on the ground of another inn. It was much like the one Paco and I were in. Only this one had no ornate carvings on the walls. The bar reminded me of a hipster joint back on Earth. Probably something you'd see on Instagram or in New York City. It was chic. I saw an open-windowed kitchen off to the side with a man by the oven. Paco sat next to me.

"Welcome to my Inn, friendsss. I'm Sly. And back there is my loyal co-hort, Jordon. He's also from Earth. I saved him many yearsss ago."

"Where are we?" I asked as I pushed myself off the floor and watched as Jordon came out of the kitchen and stood behind the bar.

"A pocket dimensssion. It allowsss me to peddle my food and drink without any interruption."

"Why bring us here then?"

"I'm alwaysss interested in new visitorsss. And with the orcsss at large, I wanted Jordon to meet people from his world."

"You really brought a dirty raccoon in here?" the man shouted at Sly.

"Behave. We have guestsss."

"What's this 'we' shit? You abducted me to cook for people. I didn't want this. And now I have to clean up after a rabies-ridden animal."

"Ignore him. He getsss moody sometimesss."

I looked over at Paco, who looked like he was about to cry.

"Chris, I don't have rabies. I'm just a little guy."

"I know. It's okay," I put my hand on Paco's back while I dug around in my pocket for a biscuit from the grays. I handed it over to Paco, who chewed on it slowly.

"Pleassse come and sssit," Sly said as he walked over to the bar.

"Come on, Paco," I said as I turned to him. He was still chewing his biscuit depressingly.

The high-top chair grated against the wooden floor with a horrific screech. I sat and watched the chair next to me slowly pull itself out. Paco climbed up and sat at the bar. He placed his biscuit down. Crumbs of it littered the spot in front of him.

I watched Jordon sigh as he picked up the biscuit, placed it on a black paper napkin, and wiped the crumbs away.

"Have anything you'd like from our menu," Sly said next to me. I tried to look under his hood, but all I could see was the twinkling of two eyes. They reminded me of diamonds glittering in the sunlight.

"What're you guys known for?" I asked.

"A little bit of this, a little bit of that. Jordon here makes the bessst coleslaw."

"Fuck you. Why would you even tell them that?" Jordon was visibly angry at the man wrapped in darkness.

"It'sss true. Our best seller."

I looked over at Paco, who had finished his biscuit. He

seemed genuinely interested in what was occurring next to us.

"One coleslaw, please," he said.

I watched Jordon sigh as he turned to me. He raised his eyebrows as he put his arm on the bar.

"Yeah, I'll do one, too."

"Great," he said with a disgusting attitude. He walked off towards the kitchen.

I turned my attention to Sly. "Now that you got us here, anything I should know?"

"No, jussst enjoy the food. Call upon me whenever you need, and we will come."

"Sounds a little suspect, honestly. Why are you being so nice to us?"

I watched the man shrug. He put his hands on the bar, and a glass of alcohol appeared before him. I watched as he put it up to his hood. The liquid disappeared instantly. When he put the glass back down, it magically refilled itself.

Jordon returned and aggressively placed two bowls of coleslaw in front of each of us. Forks clattered on the bar.

"Eat," he said.

Paco didn't say anything. I watched as he scooped some coleslaw. His eyes widened like he had fallen in love.

"This is the *best* thing I've ever had. Chris, really, you need to try it. It's better than the biscuits from the grays," he said between mouthfuls of food.

I grabbed the fork and tried it myself. It really was the best coleslaw I'd ever had. I now understood why they were known for it.

"Why do you hate making this so much? It's delicious," Paco asked.

"Doesn't matter. Hate it. Worst thing ever. I'd rather make mac and cheese." Jordon walked off again.

"So, how do we get in touch with you if we want to visit again?" I asked Sly. He had been chuckling to himself throughout the entire interaction.

"I'll be here and there. Jussst sssay my name, and I'll find you. Jordon, pleassse see our guesssts out."

Jordon returned carrying a wooden door. He stepped out from behind the bar and slammed it on the ground. It stood up without him having to hold it.

"Go on," Jordon said. "Get out. I need to clean up after that *thing*," he pointed at Paco.

Paco finished the last of his coleslaw as quickly as possible before patting himself on the stomach. I grabbed what was left of my bowl and quickly stuffed it into my inventory. I didn't think Sly would mind too much.

"Just go through the door?" I asked Sly as we walked over to it.

The hooded man nodded in return.

I pressed the handle and swung the door open. The blackness on the other side had returned. Once again, I felt the pull of eternity sucking us in.

I blinked as I sat on my ass in Wilduwen's inn. Paco was right next to me.

"Welcome back," she said from the bar. "How was your meeting with the god of chaos?"

"He was actually quite pleasant," I said.

Paco ran over and dragged himself onto the chair in front of Wilduwen.

"His cook isn't the nicest person. He called me a 'rabies-infested rat.' It really hurt my feelings. But he made us coleslaw, and it *really* was the best thing I've ever had. And then Sly said we could call on him anytime we wanted, and he'd come. I wanted to have more coleslaw, but I knew we had the feast coming up with Mr. Shoulder, and I didn't wanna be too full for it." Paco was running out of breath as he spoke.

"Yes, little one. I wouldn't trust him too much," Wilduwen said. "Anyway, the feast is going to start soon. I'm closing up shop. I did my last call already. You two should hurry along. It would be rude for our guests to be late," Wilduwen gently nudged Paco.

"Come on," I said. "Let's go see Bruk."

CHAPTER 8

PACO and I walked through the center of town towards the main building. It was pretty hard to miss, honestly. Around the square with all the merchants, there was a large building to the North. Once again, it was entirely made of wood, with intricate carvings of dwarves holding axes and shields. The main difference was in the banners that hung from some of the ramparts. Most were bright red, but there were a few that were green and others that were yellow. There was no fancy embroideries on them, just hues of color which contrasted nicely with the dark wood of the building.

We walked up the steps to the main entrance. Before we could even reach the doors, they burst open to a lot of fanfare. Music came erupting out from the inside, followed by laughter, and the raucous droning of multiple conversations all happening at the same time.

"By the ax of Lord Greatwood!" Bruk's voice boomed over

all the citizens dancing and raising their flagons. They all turned to look at us as the room fell silent. Paco ran in, and I followed him.

"Welcome, my friends.May your flagons never empty and your stomachs be full!" Brukrag raised his flagon along with everyone else. Wilduwen brought a flagon over to each of us.

Paco raised his in one hand, then produced his stick in the other. He raised the stick and shouted. "By the ax of Lord Greatwood!" he screeched.

The next moment was pure chaos. Everyone cheered and raised their flagons to their mouths. Men and women started dancing. I saw what looked like a harp being played, and another that looked to be similar to a violin. Dwarves rushed us and picked Paco up, launching him into the air. His flagon did, in fact, empty as it rained down on him and the people below. I drank from mine. It was a nice mead. Sweet and strong.

I walked through the hall, trying to avoid bumping into anyone dancing. Brukrag beckoned me to sit next to him on his left-hand side. He refilled my flagon before I even sat down.

"It is nice to have you here, my friend. By the ax of Lord Greatwood, may our swords never dull and our shields never splinter. With his fury, may the ground we walk upon give way to dust and rubble. With his patience, may the waves still and the winds fall silent in our presence. With his mercy, may our souls find peace within the earth we once emerged. Lord Greatwood, guide my hand. I am Brukrag, your humble vassal, come to this land to do thy bidding until I am once again called home. Hoy," he bowed his head. I returned the nod.

"What are those instruments called?" I asked.

"That one is called a lyre," he pointed to the man playing the instrument, which looked like a harp. "And that one is my personal favorite, the talharpa."

"I really like how they sound," I said awkwardly. I watched as Paco was repeatedly caught and tossed into the air. He was laughing each time. He still had a grip on his empty flagon, but he had put his stick back into his inventory. I could see it attached to the string on his hips, but it stuck close to his body despite the thrashing he was currently taking.

"So, uh, where should we go to level up our skills?" I asked as I started to drink more.

"There's a low-level hunting ground not far from here. You can start there and get a feel for your skills and abilities. Then we can venture out when you hit level five and take you on a real hunt," Bruk raised his flagon to me. He smashed it into the side of mine and spilled mead from both of them onto the table.

"Any advice you got?"

"I've trained many a dwarf. Once they hit their teenage years, we really start to push them. My best advice is 'don't die.'" He laughed.

"Easier said than done. We almost died to a demon hawk."

"Yeah, it's unfortunate that the Council kept your kind locked away. You'd easily be close to level one hundred by now if you had started training as a child. But what can you do?" he shrugged. "Lord Greatwood brought you here, and as a devotee, I will not let any harm come to you so long as I may live."

Paco had finally stopped being thrown into the air and stumbled over to us. He swayed back and forth as he walked, definitely from being dizzy and having his equilibrium off.

"My boy!" Brukrag shouted as he slammed an open palm on Paco's shoulder. "Please, sit down." He pulled the chair out on his right and let Paco sit down. He then filled his flagon before he had a chance to sit down.

"Thank you, Mr. Shoulder," Paco said as he lifted his flagon and took a sip. The look on his face showed pleasure rather than the disdain he had for the alcohol he received at Wilduwen's Inn.

I watched as Bruk gently patted Paco on the head, then moved his hand to his back.

"Attention, everyone! I'd like to formally begin this wondrous feast," Brukrag shouted as he stood up from his chair. Everyone in the hall immediately made their way to their seats as two long tables were dragged before us. It was like a symphony how quickly they produced an entire arrangement of utensils and plates before themselves. I watched as they all sat down and quieted, waiting for Brukrag to continue.

"Before you sit two strangers from Earth, Chris and Paco. They have traveled far among the stars, refugees in their own right. Their planet is actively engaged in a war with the orc empire." When Brukrag said this, everyone booed. "While we cannot do much to help their families and friends, the least we can do is make them comfortable as they become accustomed to their new lives as temporary members of the Council. They've already picked their classes, and had a run-in with a mother demon hawk…and survived!" Everyone cheered and raised their flagons. I turned, and Paco was doing the same. "Tomorrow I will take them to the hunting grounds as I have done with most of you. There, they will learn more about themselves. By the ax of Lord Greatwood, may our swords never dull and our shields never splinter. With his fury, may the ground we walk upon give way to dust and rubble. With his patience, may the waves still and the winds fall silent in our presence. With his mercy, may our souls find peace within the earth we once emerged. Lord Greatwood, guide my hand. I am Brukrag, your humble vassal, come to this land to do thy bidding until I am once again called home. Hoy." I bowed my head. I raised my flagon and nodded to Paco.

"By the ax of Lord Greatwood," we shouted in unison. If I thought there was chaos when Paco uttered those words before, then this was a full-on war. Before me, men and women jumped on the tables as fast as they could remove their plates. They all started cheering, screaming, and creating a ruckus that would put the largest sporting event in the world to shame.

I reached behind Brukrag and toasted Paco. "Cheers, buddy." Our flagons clinked, and we each took a sip.

Brukrag looked on as everyone celebrated our arrival. He

let this go on for a few minutes, then called for everyone to take their seats.

"Bring on the food!" he shouted. Everyone smashed their flagons together and let alcohol spill on the tables before food was swiftly brought out before them.

I watched as everyone laughed and cheered. Wilduwen brought me and Paco our own plates of food. There were roasted potatoes covered in what smelled like thyme. Carrots sauteed and caramelized with onions. The meat tasted like a mixture of pork and turkey, smothered in a rich brown gravy. It was like Thanksgiving, only amazing, and not the horribly dry turkey that everyone insisted was the best thing they ate all year. This *was* actually the best thing I ate all year. Though as I ate it, the realization hit me again. Everyone I knew was probably dead, and they would have all loved to have one more meal together, no matter how bad it truly was. Meanwhile, I was living on another planet, celebrating my own survival with a talking raccoon. I sighed.

"Survivor's guilt is okay," Brukrag said as he put a hand on my shoulder. "Just because you are alive does not mean you must feel guilt for it. The universe, Lord Greatwood, and the other gods that be have chosen you. And you should take great pride in that magnificence. You must cherish the life that you can continue to live, even if you cherish it for the people who have lost theirs. One day, you can enact your vengeance if you so wish, but today, you must celebrate life with your friends and family."

I looked over at Bruk. He had a solemn look in his eyes. "But I have no family now," I whispered.

"Nonsense," he dismissed me. "Look," he pointed ahead. Paco was in the hall talking and meandering among the dwarves. He was laughing and toasting anyone he could. "He may not be of the same race, but he is still your family. In time, you will grow to understand that. Now please eat." He raised his flagon to me.

I grabbed mine and clinked it against his.

"To cherishing life," I said.

"Ay. To cherishing life."

The next few hours were filled with more alcohol, food, and desserts than I could even comprehend. I felt stuffed, overfull, like I would throw up at any given moment. But we ate and ate until we could hardly breathe. I laughed and joked as men and women walked up to the table I sat at with Brukrag. Paco rarely came back except to bring up some background story on a random dwarf that he hardly remembered and definitely talked about way too fast to understand fully.

"Ahem!" Brukrag shouted as the desserts finished and everyone started to wind down. "It seems as though our feast is coming to a close. Soon it will be morning again. I would like to announce an official holiday for tomorrow in honor of our guests!"

Everyone cheered.

"No work! Enjoy the day as you wish and recover from this wondrous fe—" His words came to a sharp end as the main door to the hall blew open and fire rocketed towards the men and women before me.

CHAPTER 9

I LEAPT ONTO THE TABLE. The food sloshed around in my stomach. The alcohol quickly hit me, and I felt my face go numb. I put my face into my hand and smashed my **Hunter's Instinct** ability. The room changed as a soft white ping went out around me. The dwarves weren't marked, but whoever stood in the doorway was outlined in red. And there were a lot of them.

"For Lord Greatwood!" Brukrag's voice boomed through the hall. It was louder than anything I had ever heard. My ears started to ring from the massive shout that emanated from him.

A slew of buffs appeared. I felt stronger. A lot stronger. I didn't take any time to look at them. I pulled my bow and loosed arrows toward the door.

I felt Paco hop on my back. It startled me so much I

jumped and almost sent him crashing to the floor. "Sorry," I said.

"Chris, throw me!" he shouted as explosions went off again. Wood splintered and cracked as the fire spread towards us.

I didn't think. I grabbed him by the shoulder and placed a hand underneath him. I launched Paco as hard as I could towards the door. He somersaulted, landed on one of the tables, and ran on all fours towards the chaos.

I hit my **Dead Eye** ability as I knocked an arrow. It flew at what looked like a goblin. At roughly three feet tall, it had pointy ears, a long, crooked nose, and pale green skin. It was hardly wearing anything except for a tattered loincloth at the waist. It was holding a massive club, which was almost as large as itself. My arrow struck it between the eyes. It fell forward. I watched as the point came out of the back of its skull and thick black blood oozed onto the floor around it.

Men and women were now joining the fight as more goblins filled the area. Then the worst thing I heard rang in my ears. A mother demon hawk screeched as she tore through the air and landed on the table next to Paco. He was swinging his stick as hard as he could at anyone who got too close. I could just barely make out the whooshing sound it made through the explosions and yelling.

She screeched again and beat her wings, sending smoke and ash billowing around everyone. She soared up as high as the ceiling would let her go, then dove directly at Paco. I watched as her metal talons grabbed him. His stick dropped to the floor.

"No!" I shouted. "Bruk! It has Paco!"

I watched as the dwarf turned to me, then looked up to the ceiling. He pulled his ax out of the torso of a goblin and let its lifeless body flop to the floor. Before I could react, Brukrag was on me. His hands grabbed my shoulder and the back of my pants. Then I was flying again. I put my bow away and pulled my small knife. In the blink of an eye, I was thrusting it directly into the eye of the demon hawk. My body crunched as I smashed into the bird and fell back towards the floor. I felt fire burning me as I tried to blink away the pain. My bones had broken, and I could hardly breathe. I clicked my **Heal**. My health had just gotten into the red. My bones readjusted, and with every painful alignment, my consciousness slowly came back. I pushed myself off the floor and away from the fire. It whipped against me and blistered my skin.

"Where's Paco?" I shouted again. I was standing up, looking around, disoriented.

"I got him!" said a familiar voice.

"Wilduwen," I whispered.

"They're retreating!" another voice shouted. One I didn't know.

"Get the fires out!" Brukrag's voice cut through the air.

I watched as everyone swarmed in and out of the building, bringing buckets filled with water and dousing the flames. I had no clue how to help. I ran outside to the retreating throng of goblins. I ran as hard as I could towards them, eventually catching up to the injured one, who was limping away. I swung as hard as I could and felt my fingers break against the side of his skull as he let out a gasp and crashed to the ground. I was breathing heavily as I bent down, grabbed one of his spindly legs, and dragged him back towards the dwindling fire. I heard him struggling while he tried to get a hold of anything on the ground to stop me from what I was doing.

I walked up the steps, feeling the thump of his head as it connected with each step that I took. I almost felt bad. Almost. But he had been a part of this raid that almost killed me, Paco, and this community I still knew nothing about.

Inside, Paco was sitting at one of the tables with Wilduwen who was comforting him. Brukrag was up in the front directing people where to throw more water, and yelling what needed to be fixed as soon as possible. I walked up to him.

"Here," I said as I tossed the small goblin at his feet.

"What's this?"

"He's alive," I said as I focused on the goblin. It now had an **Unconscious** debuff above his head. Probably from the steps.

"You two, take him in the back," Brukrag pointed at two men who were assessing the damage to a few of the wooden beams. They quickly obliged, and the goblin was taken away. Before they disappeared behind a door, I was able to finally focus on it and get more details.

Goblin. Level 8. It's nothing special. Carries around a big club to make up for its overall size. Yes, that size is included. It's small. Comically so. That's why they're so

angry all the time, and their women are unfulfilled. That being said, don't get into too much trouble with them. A goblin raid—or their counterparts, the hobgoblins—are nothing to be fucked with. They like fire. They like explosions, and they get off on the chaos of both. Usually seen riding demon hawks.

Interesting, I thought. I wondered if killing that first baby was the reason they came here. But how would they even know? A tracker? A pet? Something that didn't come back when it was supposed to? Like a child who was supposed to be home when the streetlights came on.

"How are you feeling?" I asked as I walked over to Paco.

"Pretty good, still a bit sore. Wilduwen had to heal me because I was unconscious when we fell. And a patch of my fur is gone." He turned to show me where the massive metal talons dug into his side just below the ribs.

"Another cool scar?" I asked.

"No," Paco said sullenly. "Wilduwen said the healing spell she cast on me will fully mend anything. And my hair will grow back. No scar this time."

I noticed Paco had leveled up. He was now close to level seven. I checked mine and saw I was just barely level six.

"Oh, cool, we both leveled up with that. I also got a box for stabbing the demon hawk in the eye. What'd you get?"

Paco took a moment.

"I got a box for surviving the attack and another box for almost dying." There was a brief pause. "And my stick leveled up!" Paco stood up and produced the stick.

Upgraded Lackluster Stick of the Samurai.

"What's that mean?"

"Watch," he said as the stick sat on his waist. He grabbed the top just above the lone leaf that clung to the side. He pulled, and out came a sword. It made that classic sound from every movie I'd ever seen, and when he swung it, it still made the whooshing sound he loved.

"Fuck," I whispered. He was going to hurt himself or someone else.

"Isn't it cool?!"

"Yeah," I said. "It sure is."

He put the sword away, and it made the same movie sound as he sheathed it.

"Good job, you two," Brukrag said as he came over. "It has been a while since I've seen someone so low-level take out a mother that big," he said as he turned towards the corpse of the bird.

"Can I loot it?" Paco asked.

"Yes, but Chris gets first pick since it was his kill," Bruk turned and nodded at me.

I walked over to the bird and looted all of the meat and feathers. I left the rest for Paco. Even leaving a surprise for him.

Paco scampered over when I was done. "Why'd you leave these?" he asked.

"I knew you'd want them."

Paco pulled the metal talons from the bird's feet as blood splashed onto the floor. "Thank you, Chris." He nodded as he put the talons away.

"Now, it's time to go question our guest. Come," Brukrag said as he led us to a room behind where we had sat at the feast.

CHAPTER 10

WE FOLLOWED BEHIND BRUKRAG, who stoically marched into the room. The two dwarves closed the wooden doors behind us with a fierce *shunk*. It felt as if the air pressure had blown the door closed. My arm hair stood up, and I felt the goosebumps form.

Paco and I stood side by side. I looked over; his paw was on the hilt of his newly formed sword. I wondered what it would turn into when he leveled it up more. I feared it even. He looked at me, nodded, then turned back to Brukrag who stood in front of the goblin.

The goblin seemed smaller than when I first saw it. His hands were bound in rope and tied behind the chair it sat in. The ropes twisted and wound themselves around his chest. I could see they were already digging into his skin and leaving depressions between his ribs. *Damn, those are tight.* I saw that his loincloth was now soiled. A ring was on his left hand.

"What's your name?" Brukrag's voice was low and filled with primordial rage.

The goblin looked up, one of his eyes swollen shut. It hadn't been like that when I punched him in the side of the head, at least, I didn't remember causing it. I assumed he was beaten when he was dragged back here and tied up. It didn't matter to me. He had been a part of the plot to kill all of us, and he deserved it. I sighed at the thought. I no longer felt like myself. I felt like a monster for having the thought in the first place. But I had almost died. Paco was even closer to that end than I was, and our hosts now had to rebuild this place because of what had happened. I shook my head and watched the two talk.

The goblin said nothing. He spat a mucousy green blob onto the floor. There was a red shimmer to parts of it, and when it hit, there was a small clatter as one of his teeth also came out.

"I said, what's your name?" Brukrag growled again. There was no answer. "No matter, I'll get my answer," he said as he pulled back his fist and slammed it into the liver of the goblin. Air escaped his lungs, and the goblin coughed. He muttered something.

"What was that?" Brukrag asked as he leaned closer.

"It's Steven," the goblin rasped.

"Ah. Steven. I am Brukrag, and these fine folk behind me are Chris and Paco. Guests whose celebratory dinner you crashed and ruined."

"I know of 'em," Steven said as he glared up at us.

"Oh? Do inform me," Brukrag looked down at the creature.

"Killed one of me birds. No reason fer it. Just out there. Killed the little thing 'fore it knew what 'appened."

"Your birds?"

"Yer. Been raisin' 'em since they were chicks. Born of fire, die of fire. That's the way these things are supposed to 'appen."

"We could have settled this peacefully," Brukrag said. His voice was solemn. "But *you* launched an attack on us. And I cannot let that go." The rage in his voice was building.

"What about the treaty?" Steven asked as he looked up at Brukrag. There was a sly grin on his face.

"There is no treaty now. You attacked us and our guests, who had not learned the ways of this planet. We could have brokered a deal, and I would have obliged. I had not known that the baby and the mother were your property."

"Without the treaty, what about the dragons?" The smirk became even wider.

"Ay, the dragons. Looking for **The Great Biscuit Recipe**. Peace among our people. Do not worry your little head about such matters. I will send you back to your people in pieces!" he shouted. Brukrag pulled his ax.

Before I could say anything, Paco was across the room, sword in hand. He slashed down and cut Steven's fingers . The ring fell to the floor as the goblin screeched.

"No," Brukrag said sternly. "This does not concern you, little one."

"Yes, it does, Mr. Shoulder. They almost killed me, and I have the marks to prove it until they fully heal," Paco said as he turned to show where the talons of the demon hawk dug into him.

"That is not how things are done around here," Brukrag said.

"Forgive me. But where I come from, I also hold this right. I have been disrespected and almost killed. What would Lord Greatwood think about that?" Paco shot back as he sheathed his sword.

Brukrag appeared pensive for a moment. He then nodded. "Ay. Lord Greatwood would allow it. As guests, it is my job to defend you and your honor, though I am also responsible for your mistakes. But I do not know the ways of your people, and I have forgotten that. Please, forgive me," Brukrag said as he stepped back and outstretched his arm. "You may proceed."

Paco looked over at me, then winked. "Thank you, Mr. Shoulder. For understanding that our ways are different from yours. I am sorry if this has caused a stain here for your people. I only wanted what vengeance was rightfully mine. I will take these as a token," Paco bent down and scooped up the fingers of the goblin and his ring. "I will allow you to handle the rest of this situation as you seem fit for your people."

Brukrag grunted in acceptance.

"We will head to our home now," Paco said as he crossed the room towards me.

"I will see you two tomorrow," Brukrag said before turning back to Steven.

"For Lord Greatwood," Paco said as the two dwarves opened the doors for us.

"For Lord Greatwood!" Brukrag's voice bellowed before the doors closed behind us. I swore I could hear the sound of his ax as it connected with a part of the goblin's body. I hoped it was his head, so the death was quick and clean. But I knew the answer to that.

"You played it cool back there," I said.

"Yeah, I wasn't sure if it would work. But I wanted this ring." Paco held up the small gold ring and let it shimmer in the firelight as we stepped back into the town.

"What about the fingers?"

"Those were just a bonus." Paco put the ring away.

"What're you collecting all of this stuff for, anyway?" I asked. I thought it was weird. He now had the skull of a baby demon hawk, the fingers of a goblin, the talons of a mother, and the teeth of a snake.

"Don't worry about it. I have plans, and when I have what I need, you'll see."

I gave him a look, but didn't respond. He was planning something weird; I just knew it.

We walked inside our new home. There was a familiar smell to it this time. A sort of nostalgia for the place I used to live. Only now I had a talking raccoon who I couldn't decide if he was a psychopath or neurotic. Probably both. Either way, he was still good company, even if I didn't know what he was going to do or steal next. I watched as he didn't say a word, simply walked over to his "door" and disappeared into his room. I walked to mine.

The wave of nostalgia hit me again as I opened the door and saw everything I once loved and worked for. I loved and hated it all at once. Memories flooded me as I relived all the moments I once had here. Now, on this foreign planet, I hated everything that I saw in front of me. I started editing my new home in a fervor.

The bed became twice as large; the sheets changed from white to black. The sliding glass windows, which looked out onto the world, disappeared into tiny things you'd see in a basement. The dresser, which housed a TV that didn't work, disappeared and was replaced by a modern standing wardrobe, which was also black. The lamps were replaced with standing floor LEDs, which changed color.

When I was finished, it didn't feel like the home I knew, but the home I needed. Something different, something foreign, that I would grow accustomed to.

I do like the renovating you're doing. Very chic. Probably the first and only compliment you'll get from me.

"Thanks," I said to the AI as I walked over and plopped myself down onto my new bed. The fatigue of the day instantly washed away as I stared at the ceiling and disappeared into the realm between life and death.

I woke to a knock on my door.

"Chris, get up," Paco's squeaky voice came from beyond the door. "Brukrag wants to take us out hunting today!"

"I'm coming," I said as I sat up and rubbed the sleep from

my eyes. I grabbed my bow, which rested next to my end table, and grabbed my knife from it. I had no clue what time it was, but I still felt tired, nonetheless. Although the fatigue had washed itself away when I lay down, it still persisted deep inside me. I could sleep for years and still not be satisfied. I opened the door.

Paco stood there, his stick in hand, waiting for me. I nodded, and we walked outside.

Brukrag stood there stoically. On his back was the ax I knew he had used to slay the goblin hostage. A sense of dread radiated from it, and the air between us became thick with tension.

"By the ax of Lord Greatwood, it is good to see you two, though it is later than I would have liked. Paco says you slept most of the morning."

"What time is it?" I looked up toward the sky. The sun was almost entirely overhead.

"Just about noon. No matter, we will go to the training grounds and get you two ready." I watched as Brukrag turned and began walking to the far end of town, away from the gates we had come through in the War Wagon.

"Mr. Shoulder, what can we expect to fight when we're there?" Paco asked.

"Nothing too crazy. A few boars, maybe some snakes. The golems are nearby, but they generally don't venture onto the training grounds. You may come across some baby wolves," Brukrag replied.

"I hope we get some boar," Paco said.

I knew exactly why. It was so obvious. "What about these

golems?" I asked. "Are they like the ones we heard about on Earth?"

"I do not know the history of golems on Earth," Brukrag replied. "Please inform me."

"They're made entirely of rock. Sometimes they can control the ground you walk on and make pillars of stone erupt from beneath your feet. That's the general consensus," I explained.

"Ay. That's pretty close. They are made entirely of rock and control the ground we walk on to an extent. Their blood is made of lava, so be sure not to get burned. They're weak in the cracks between the stony skin," Brukrag said.

We walked out through the gate of the town and marched along the road for what felt like an hour. I watched as the sun slid through the sky, and the scent of cooked meat and mead slowly faded away. It was replaced with the musk of nature and the distinct smell of rain in spring.

CHAPTER 11

THE HUNTING GROUNDS were an open field littered with little white flowers. The trees were barely existent here, but in the far-off distance, you could see shades of pink. Beyond, there was a towering mountain spewing smoke and ash.

"What's that?" Paco asked as he pointed.

"The home of dragons. Created during the time of Lord Greatwood. It releases smoke and ash, spews lava, but the wind takes it away from us thanks to Lord Greatwood's blessing and sacrifice."

"How was it 'created' during his time?" Paco looked up at Brukrag inquisitively.

I watched as Brukrag looked down at Paco with a pensive stare, deciding if he wanted to talk about this right now.

"Let me shorten it for you so we can hunt. Then, later, I will tell you the full story. Lord Greatwood united the dwarves of old under his house banner as the golems encroached on multiple territories all at once. They were led by Krik-krak the Obsidianblade. With their forces united, Lord Greatwood was able to repel the golem attacks, albeit with heavy losses. Eventually, he marched to Srazada-um, which is the mountain you see in the distance. Lord Greatwood and Krik-krak waged battle for a fortnight until both succumbed to their injuries. Lord Greatwood was then granted access to the Gates of Valhalla, where he resides until Krik-krak's return. Then, the gates will open, and his ax shall fall once again on Krik-krak."

"Wait, so this obsidian guy is going to come back even though he died? Same with Lord Greatwood?" Paco's eyes were full of wonder in the legend that Brukrag was telling.

Brukrag put his hand on Paco's head. "Do not worry, little one. I will explain it all, eventually. I do believe it is now time to hunt."

Paco turned to me and rubbed his hands together. I sighed, went into my inventory, and produced a biscuit for him as Brukrag started jogging into the field of white flowers.

"Go as fast as you can!" he shouted back to us.

I ran, my feet pushing hard against the ground. Before I could even cover the ground Brukrag put between us, I felt myself breathing heavily. Paco, on the other hand, had almost caught up to him. I slowed and began to jog, trying to catch my breath. I looked up and saw Brukrag had stopped, and Paco was still running in circles around him, laughing.

"You need to work on your cardio," Bruk said. I bent over, put my hands on my knees, and tried to slow my breathing.

"You have hidden abilities that aren't directly tied to everything else you're able to upgrade. These will automatically upgrade as you use them."

"What kind of abilities?" Paco asked as he continued to run around.

"Swimming, running, things you barely think you use."

Don't forget coordination. The dexterity in your fingers and hands. Flexibility. Jumping. Shit like that, the AI chirped in as Brukrag laughed. It had been a while since we had heard its voice. It was startling at first.

"It's been a while since someone has spoken to me that way," Brukrag said.

"Yeah, well, I'm used to it. This thing hates me." I showed him the sleeve as I finally started to recover my breath.

"So, does that mean things like climbing? I'm already pretty good at that," Paco finally came to a stop.

"I'm sure you're already decently leveled in it, but yes, you can continue to increase these hidden abilities just by existing. Remember, especially you," Brukrag pointed at me, "you have to get these things leveled up. Laziness will be the death of you in times of war. They can decrease over time, though that is infrequent. If you become sloth-like, your cardio and running will go down. Now that you're a part of the Council, you will be able to run faster than the fastest animal on your planet should you choose to train and push yourself beyond your perceived limits."

"Understood," I said. I looked over at Paco, who simply saluted Brukrag after he finished speaking. He stood there waiting for something to happen.

"Alright, now let's get to work," Brukrag said. "I want you guys to work on climbing and ambushing any little animals you find. There should be boars beyond this line of trees in a clearing. They like to graze around this time."

I followed Paco as quickly as I could as he scurried off towards the tree line. He scampered up a tree. I climbed up behind him as best I could, grabbing any limb that wouldn't break under my weight. More than once the thought crossed my mind that the wood would snap and I'd go tumbling back down to the ground, which seemed to be a common occurrence these last few days. When I finally caught up to Paco, he was staring at a group of boars. There were four just chilling in the patch of grass, snorting as they ate anything they could get their mouths on. I inspected them. They were all level seven.

"Okay, so what's the plan, Chris?"

"I think I'm going to use **Deadeye**, then I'll hit one or two of them. You should go to another tree quietly. Then you can jump down and use **Double Slash** on any that get away."

Paco nodded in return before he took off and made his way around to another tree. I could barely see him as he camouflaged against the bark. He waved his stick, and I could see the green flash of the leaf through the pink. I looked down at the closest boar and activated **Deadeye**.

My knocked arrow loosed after I drew back the bow and paused to steady my breath. It aimed true and connected with the animal just behind the ribs. The squealing was horrendous as it lashed out and ran away from where I sat. I knocked another arrow, steadied my bow, and launched it at a boar that had looked up to see what the fuss was about. I missed as my arrow dug into the ground next to it.

"Shit," I whispered as my hands fumbled for another arrow. This one hit its mark and connected with the head of the boar. Before it knew what had happened, it collapsed onto the ground. The others had now taken notice and began to run away with the bleeding pig.

I watched as Paco jumped from the tree and pulled his sword from the sheath. He plunged directly down onto one. The metal went straight through the animal as Paco stabbed it in the back. I watched as the handle dug into Paco's chest, and a sickly groan escaped him. His health bar had gone down by half, and I knew the maneuver was meant to look cool, but he hadn't thought it through. Inertia had taken over, and his arms weren't strong enough to stop the handle from pushing back into his ribs.

I quickly slid down the tree and ran over to Paco. He had used **Heal**. I could hear his ribs clicking back into place like little twigs snapping.

"That one really hurt," he groaned as he pulled his sword from the boar.

"Yeah, it wasn't the brightest idea, but it worked. You got the kill." I kicked the lifeless form at our feet.

"Where are the others?" he asked.

"Gotta go find the one I injured, but I think one of them got away."

"Okay, go get the blood trail. I'm gonna loot this guy." Paco sheathed his sword, and it made that classic movie sound again. I watched as he bent over the boar and started tugging on its tusks. I had no clue what he was planning, but my deranged party member was damned sure he was going to do it. I said nothing as I looked to the ground for the blood trail.

It wasn't hard to find. I followed the glistening red puddles away from my tree. My bow was now on my back, and my knife in hand. I figured it would be a quicker end when I came across the animal.

Maybe fifty yards away, I found it. The boar was panting as it began to drown in its own blood. It was sad, really. I felt a pang of guilt. I had never hunted anything before. As I stood above the furry brown pig, I saw the terror in its eyes.

"I'm sorry," I whispered as I knelt down and put my knife to its throat where I thought a vein or artery would be. I hesitated, but knew it was worse to let it suffer. The tip of my knife went to its throat, and I put my hand on the back of the handle and jammed it in. There was a squeal of pain as blood squirted out. I watched as its eyes dilated and the vacancy of death took hold of it before I pulled my knife from its throat. I wiped the blood off on its fur and looted it.

I had gotten a few pieces of raw boar meat and a tattered leather hide. I walked back to Paco, who was already looting my other kill.

"Got what I needed," he said as he showed me four boar tusks. "Did you get them from the other one?" he asked.

"No, just some meat and a hide."

I watched as he shook his head. "Let's get back to Mr. Shoulder."

Brukrag was waiting for us. "How did it go?"

"Paco got hurt a little, but we killed three boars."

"Not bad for your first hunt," he laughed. "What happened to your little friend?" Brukrag looked at Paco.

"I jumped from a tree and slashed down at a boar. The handle of my sword hit me in the ribs when I impaled it, and it broke some things in me. But I healed myself, and I'm all better now," Paco said as he rubbed his sternum.

"Flashy isn't always a good thing, little one. I'm just glad you aren't seriously hurt. The rearranging of bones always gave me a sickly feeling."

"Yeah, I didn't really like how it felt," Paco said as he sat down. "I think I'm gonna have a little snack now. Chris and I are almost level eight after that."

I watched as Paco produced a biscuit and started munching on it.

"Where'd you get that one?" I asked.

Paco looked up to me and didn't answer. I checked my inventory. All of the biscuits were gone.

"You stole them from me!"

Paco laughed. "Gotta pay more attention, Chris. I might be a Samurai class, but I am still a thief."

I rolled my eyes. It didn't actually bother me. I was worried about how easily he had done it, though I knew he wouldn't steal maliciously from me. Would he? I shook the thought from my head. I sat down. Brukrag joined us.

"Where to next?" I asked.

"Probably head back to town then come—" There was a honking noise. It reminded me of the laughter of the grays. I watched as Brukrag quickly became alert and turned to face something behind us.

"We need to go," he said firmly as he stood up and wielded his ax.

"What, why?" Paco said, still sitting on the ground.

I looked over and saw it.

Anomalous Spirit of the Goose. Level 1. Don't fuck with this thing. I mean it. It's only level 1, but it will totally fuck you up. Leave any bread on the ground and just back away slowly. These things want one thing and one thing only. And you have it. Don't try to befriend it. It always ends badly when the goose is loose. You might think, "Oh, but I'm different. Surely I can tame this thing." No, you can't. To think so is a fool's dream. When these guys are mad, they grow to be as tall as mountains and grow heads like hydras. They'll blast you to Hell with fire magic, cool you down with ice, then, when your heart stops beating, they'll shock you back to life just to do it again.

"But I want my biscuit!" Paco screeched.

"Didn't you hear what your foot bracelet said!" I shouted back as I grabbed him like a toddler throwing a temper tantrum. He dropped his biscuit from the force. I threw Paco over my shoulder as the goose started racing towards us.

"Back to town now!" Brukrag shouted.

I was already at full sprint as Paco struggled on my shoulder. I heard the thunderclap of Brukrag's footfall behind us. The honking grew louder, then it stopped entirely. I quickly turned my head to see the goose scarfing down the biscuit and flapping its white wings. It reminded me more of a swan than anything, but I didn't want to argue with the AI's description.

I didn't stop running until I could see the town. I was entirely out of breath, and my neck was thrashed from Paco clawing me to get free. He had finally given up when he realized he'd never be able to break my grip on him, no matter how hard he tried. I put him down.

"Sorry," I said.

"Don't," Paco replied as he turned his back on me and started walking towards the gate.

"He'll be fine," Brukrag said as he came up behind me and put his hand on my shoulder.

"Yeah, he's just... I don't know. He's like a child sometimes."

"Because he *is* a child. He's scared of the world around him. He was taken from his home just like you and given intelligence he never asked for. He's living for the first time just like you. Just give him time. He'll be fine."

"You're right. Let's get back home," I said. *Home.* What a foreign word.

CHAPTER 12

BRUKRAG LEFT us to go back to his home and watch over the reconstruction effort. Paco walked in front of me the entire way back to ours, but not once did he turn back or talk to me. He was down and depressed over a single biscuit, which I thought was stupid, but I tried not to dwell on it too much. He'd be fine. I'd find a way to make it up to him at some point.

We walked inside. I laid my bow and knife on the table in our living space. I watched as Paco walked over to his manhole cover.

"Hey, I'm gonna go out into the town for a bit," I said. He didn't respond to me. I let the moment settle. Paco stood there. I watched as he decided whether he wanted to say anything. He didn't. His paws reached down and grabbed his door. He lifted it from the floorboards. "I'm sorry. I just didn't want you to die," I said abruptly. The manhole cover closed, and I walked back out into the town.

The sun was setting. I quickly made my way to the center of town as the clouds turned shades of purple and orange. Torches flickered in the coming darkness. The air was warm, like a nice spring night just before the sweltering summer came. When the wind picked up, I felt like I could almost use a jacket. Almost.

I passed by a few vendors, some of whom looked familiar. I'd probably seen their faces at Brukrag's feast. Some sold fruit, others dried meats; one or two of them were selling clothes, which caught my eye. I decided against them all. I wasn't built to wear dwarf clothes. I'd have to learn to make my own, which I was sure was a trait or ability I could level up. Then I wondered if I could make armor, and even enchant it. That would be something I brought up with Brukrag eventually.

The little row of stalls was still crowded as I turned to the main square of the town. I meandered through, most people leaving me alone as I did. Then, I had a bright idea. And probably the dumbest one I could think of. I tucked myself into an alley. No one walked by as I cloaked myself in darkness.

"Sly, I need you," I whispered.

A door appeared on the wall in front of me. I opened it. The empty void stood in front of me, and I stepped through.

This time, I landed on my feet as I felt the pull of the universe grip the hair on my arms and pores on my face. Sly was sitting at the bar with Jordon.

"Nice to sssee you again."

"Thanks," I said.

"What isss it you need?" Sly's cloaked head turned to me.

"I need something to make Paco feel better. He's pretty mad at me. I figured I could get some coleslaw to go, and then maybe make a trade?"

I watched as Jordon sighed. "I'm gonna fucking kill myself if I have to keep making this trash."

"No, you aren't," Sly replied.

I watched as Jordon pulled out a knife. "I'm really gonna do it this time," he said.

Sly quickly snapped his fingers, and the knife disappeared.

I laughed at the interaction, but felt guilty about it at the same time. Jordon was a hostage in his own right, but he wasn't dead. I wondered if I could bargain for his freedom at some point. I knew Sly would ask a heavy price for it.

"Go get some colessslaw."

Jordon sighed and walked to the kitchen.

"What do you have for trade?" Sly asked.

"Not a whole lot. I have a tattered hide from a boar, and all of this meat from the animals we killed." I pulled up my inventory and let the wet meat splatter onto the bar. I knew that was going to piss off Jordon when he came back. The tattered hide covered the mess for the most part.

"I believe I can make some ussse of this. At least for hisss sssake," the cloaked hood motioned towards Jordon in the kitchen.

"I'll take whatever you can give me as long as this covers it and coleslaw too," I said.

"Deal." Sly snapped his fingers, and the pile of meat disappeared along with the tattered leather.

In its place was a massive stinger. It looked like it had come off a prehistoric scorpion. I quickly grabbed it and shoved it into my inventory just as Jordon came back and placed a to-go box in front of me. I opened it to make sure. I nodded.

"Can you send me back to the house?"

"Of courssse," Sly said. Jordon went back into the kitchen and carried the wooden door out without saying a word.

"Thank you," I said as I turned the knob and stepped through the void once more.

I was standing outside of the house. The moon was in full glow now, and I wondered how much time had actually passed. It seemed like time moved differently wherever Sly lived. Almost as if he could slow down or speed it up at will. I stepped inside, went to my room, and crashed on my bed.

———

I woke to a knock at my door. I quickly got up and opened the door. Brukrag greeted me.

"Good morning, Chris. I have something to show you and Paco," he said.

I peered over his shoulder. Paco was sitting on the sofa. Still, he did not even look at me.

"Okay, but can you give us a moment?"

Brukrag nodded, turned, and walked outside.

I sat across from Paco.

"Hey, I really am sorry about yesterday. I got you some things to make up for it." I watched as his tiny ears twitched and he gave me a sideways glance. "First, I want you to have this." I produced the to-go container of coleslaw and left it on the table.

"Thank you," he said as he leaned forward, grabbed it, and started eating. I watched some life come back into his eyes as he enjoyed the food.

"And then I got you this," I said as I stood up and moved away from the table.

The scorpion stinger clunked to the floor. It had to be at least three feet long.

"Holy shit," Paco's mouth was agape as he spoke. He even dropped the box he ate from and let the cabbage fly all over the floor. He walked over and ran his hands over the stinger. "It's still sharp," he said as he touched the point at the end. "Did you kill this yesterday?"

"No. I made a trade with Sly last night."

"Chris, really. This more than makes up for my lost biscuit. Thank you," he ran over and hugged my leg. There were tears in his eyes, I noticed.

"I don't know what you're doing with all the things you take, but if I can help, I will." I ran my hand over his head. "Now, get this thing put away, and your coleslaw, then meet me outside. I don't want to keep Bruk waiting."

Paco nodded and dragged the scorpion stinger down into his room. I waited outside while he cleaned up.

I walked outside to see Brukrag, who only nodded when I came out. We both stood there, waiting in silence for Paco. Eventually, he opened the door and closed it quietly.

"Ready?" Paco asked.

I nodded before I looked over to Brukrag, who grunted in return. We both followed him into town.

"So, what was that thing yesterday?" Paco asked.

"The goose?" Brukrag wanted to confirm.

"Yeah, what was that about? It was only level one."

"That thing is the stuff of nightmares. A god-killer who refuses to ascend to the celestial plane. Rare. Extremely rare. So rare that I'd never seen one in person. The stories are passed down from generation to generation."

"The celestial plane? And what stories?" Paco looked up to Brukrag as we found ourselves in the square. Everyone was out in full force today. Buying, selling, trading, talking. It seemed like a festival was going on, but this time, no one really paid us any mind.

"The Celestial Plane is where the gods live. The good and the bad. And yes, it is different from Valhalla. Valhalla is where all the dead gods go. The Celestial Plane is like a massive city, or so it's said. No mortal may enter. No mortal may leave. The last known anomalous goose in recorded history was after Lord Greatwood—bless his soul—fought Krik-krak. It became so enraged at not getting a piece of the Great Biscuit that it leveled entire mountains and unleashed a maelstrom of tornadoes coated with fire and lightning before raising the oceans to drown the villages. It's said that goose took out an entire continent in less than a fortnight."

"Do you think we all just imagined it? You know, being out in the sun the entire time? Maybe we all lost our minds for a bit."

"I would hope to believe that, though I do not have as much optimism as you on the subject, little one. The histories say that one day the goose will return and the Dragon King will die. When that happens, our people will be free, but chaos will blanket the world. Sulfur and hellfire will rise and block out the sun. The world will go dark, and we will have to stay in our homes. Only the righteous devotees of Lord Greatwood will survive the second coming of the anomalous goose."

"Are you going to tell everyone about the goose?" Paco asked. "You know, so they can prepare?"

I watched as Brukrag took a deep breath and held it.

"No," he replied. "If I were wrong, and that was not the anomalous goose, then I would create a panic for my people that would surely destroy them all. Besides, I need everyone focused on the current task at hand. I suggest you not bring up the goose in public or to anyone besides me and Chris. Now come, I have something to show you both."

We were standing outside the hall where our feast had quickly ended. The wood had been repaired as if nothing had happened. Brukrag opened the doors for us, and we followed through the long room before taking a staircase that led down.

CHAPTER 13

WE FOLLOWED Brukrag through a series of locked doors, all of which were made of iron instead of the wood that I had known the town to be made of. At the base of a winding staircase, we came to one last doorway that reached at least twenty feet high.

"It's cold down here. How deep are we exactly?" I asked as I looked around and noticed the walls were chiseled rock.

"We are a few hundred feet below the surface," Brukrag replied as he stepped up to the massive doors. They reminded me more of the bulkheads on the gray's ship than anything.

He took his ax in his hand and slotted it between the two. There was a crunching sound that reverberated against the rocks and back to my ears. It made my head spin. I clasped my hands to my head to try to drown out the sound as I watched Brukrag's ax glow neon green. It came from the blade and wound its way around the head down the wooden shaft. Brukrag grabbed the handle and pulled the ax from the door. Each door slid open as he did so.

Inside, there were lanterns, which helped us see better. I could just make out a faint outline of something big in the distance.

"This," he said as he waved his arm forward and begged us to enter, "this is what we will use to fight Squish the Goblin King for his attack on our home."

Paco and I walked further inside as more lanterns seemingly lit themselves with what I could only assume to be dwarven magic. Paco gasped as the lanterns behind the figure finally showed us what it was.

It was a mech made entirely of wood and iron. On one shoulder sat a cannon, or maybe it was a Gatling gun. There were three tubes lined up next to each other. The cylinders were easily four feet wide. One of its arms had an ax for a hand, and the other was a regular arm with a hand made of wood. It was compact for its height. Wider than it should have been, rather than tall and long. In the center, I could see a cockpit behind the lone piece of glass.

"You guys built this?" Paco screeched as he ran up to take a closer look.

"Yes, this is my doing. This is my mech. I will sit inside and unleash the rage Lord Greatwood once brought down on his enemies."

"I didn't know you guys made bullets," I said.

"We do not. When the time comes, you will see how the

gun works. In the meantime, please take a closer look. I think you, little one, will appreciate this most of all."

I watched as Paco turned back to face us, nodded, and climbed all around the wooden mech.

"How do I get in the cockpit?" he shouted across to us.

Brukrag didn't answer. He walked over and pulled his ax back from his shoulders, the white pelt flowing as he did. He banged the ax on the floor, and the mech knelt down in front of Brukrag. The cockpit opened, and Brukrag jumped inside. The cockpit remained open.

"Please join me," he said to Paco, who was already climbing down from the gun to get a look at the controls.

I walked closer to the hulking mech as I watched Paco rummage around the cockpit as Brukrag sat in the pilot's seat. I ran my hands over the legs. The wood was smooth. Almost like there was a varnish on it. It was almost slippery to the touch. The ax blade was cool, and its edge sliced my finger when I touched it. I sucked the blood off and pressed my finger to my pant leg to stop the bleeding. It wasn't deep, but it didn't want to stop. I looked up at the two in the cockpit.

"How do I get up there?" I asked.

"There's a ladder in the back," Brukrag's voice boomed down to me. I walked around and found an iron ladder and climbed up to find rungs going toward the gun, and another set which looped around to the front.

I stepped inside the cockpit and found it more spacious than it seemed on the outside. There was another chair facing the rear of the mech. Against the back wall, there were gauges, levers, and buttons to press.

"What is all that?" I asked.

"Gotta keep an eye on the engine when this thing is fully powered. Make sure nothing catches fire and pressure doesn't build up in the skeleton."

"What powers it? I don't see a furnace," I said.

"Dwarven magic," Brukrag said as he lifted his ax and placed it into a slot on his left. All of these gauges lifted, and a small orange light lit up the cockpit. The mech lurched, and I almost lost my balance.

"This is awesome!" Paco yelled.

"So, you guys know magic, too?" I asked.

"We do. But it's reserved for leaders and descendants of Lord Greatwood. We don't often use it. It is better to fight your foes head-on than from a high tower. Then you can see them off to Valhalla personally."

"I see," I muttered. I wondered if Brukrag saw me as a coward for choosing the Ranger class. I figured that was why he took such a liking to Paco. He was an up-close and personal fighter, something that was honored in their culture. I tried not to dwell on it too much, but his words made me feel like an outcast, even though they had treated me with nothing but hospitality.

I stood there looking around as Brukrag showed Paco what the controls did. The mech moved forward and back. The ax swung. The fingers grabbed. I felt myself disassociate from this foreign world and long for my true home again, even though I knew it probably no longer remained. I swore I was dreaming when I came here, and now I found this was no longer a dream. It was my life, my nightmare, and I had to find some comfort in it knowing I'd probably never see anyone or anything from my old life except for Paco.

"So, when are you guys going to fight this Squish guy?" I asked, trying to find a way into the conversation.

"You are coming with us. So is Paco," Brukrag said.

I gulped. We had barely survived the last attack by small goblins and the demon hawk. Now we were going to be a part of a war that had nothing to do with us. Or maybe it had everything to do with us being here. I couldn't come to a conclusion on the matter and didn't want to bring it up with Brukrag.

"When is the attack?" I asked.

"It'll be in two days," Brukrag's voice was cold.

"Don't you think we're a bit under-leveled for this?" Paco asked, saving me the same thought.

"Yes. But you fared well against the demon hawk and goblins. You two will be on our backline. I will be with the vanguard leading the assault. At most, you'll have to deal with some flyers, maybe a trebuchet or two. Don't worry, there will be a mage with you two to cast a shield over you. Think of it as a way to farm XP and level up rather than being involved in the brutal fighting. That's my job. Afterwards, we will celebrate as we were supposed to. This time with no distractions." Brukrag turned to face me and Paco. He had now jumped onto my shoulder. His eyes were piercing, and I felt a chill go down my spine.

"Okay," I said as me and Paco nodded. There was a nervous energy between us, but we felt slightly comforted by having protection.

"Good," he said as he lifted his ax from the slot and powered down the mech. "Now let's get some rest. Tomorrow, you can stock up on potions. We'll probably have a piece of leftover armor for each of you. It's not much, but it'll give you a buff. Please feel free to keep it as a token of my gratitude."

CHAPTER 14

I WOKE to find Paco waiting in our living room. He was eating the coleslaw I had gotten him. His shoulders were scrunched in on his chest, and he looked over to our little fireplace, which we had never lit.

"Morning," I said.

He looked up at me. His eyes were wide and already on the brink of tears. He was clearly nervous, but he still ate in silence. I sat down across from him.

"Are you ready for tomorrow?" I asked.

"Not really," he replied as he placed his bowl of coleslaw down on the table in front of him. "I don't want to get hurt again, Chris. That demon hawk almost killed me."

"But, it didn't. And we're stronger now."

"Yeah, but how strong are we? Sure, Mr. Shoulder has defenses for us, but will that matter in war? What if our mage doesn't protect us? Or worse, he leaves us to save himself. I'm worried. I mean, I trust Mr. Shoulder, but I don't know anyone else here besides you."

I felt my face become pensive. I didn't have any words to comfort him. I felt the same way. There was so much going on, and no time to deal with it. Tomorrow we'd be marching off to war and fighting alongside people we didn't even know. I heard a ping and scrolled through my menus.

"Hey, I got some achievements and a new quest!" Paco said. He must have gotten the same notifications I did.

New Achievement: Discover a secret you should not know about.

Congrats. Brukrag Oakshoulder showed you his hidden mech. No one outside of the royal bloodline knows about it, but for whatever reason, he chose you two to be the first. There's something special in that. I don't know what it is. Gratitude? Maybe you should show it. Anyway, here's your lootbox.

"I got an Uncommon Iron Lootbox of the Royal Bloodline," I said.

"I did, too."

New Achievement: Get dragged into geopolitics you have no business in. Awesome. You decided it was a good idea to force your way into a culture you know nothing about; now you have to deal with the repercussions. You're like a teenager on the internet, making videos telling people what their opinions should be. Self-righteous asshole. Go to war with them now. Maybe then you can have an opinion on what they're doing here.

"Uh, okay. That one was weird. I didn't really have any

opinions about it. And I didn't force my way in. I got thrown in because aliens abducted me."

They saved your life. Don't argue semantics with me. Enjoy your lootbox.

"Rare Iron Lootbox of the Self-Righteous. Nice."

"Mine isn't that mean," Paco said.

"Yeah, well, the AI the grays gave us hates me. But whatever, it's free loot. I got one more. It's a quest," I said as I scrolled through the menu. I laughed.

New Quest: Don't die tomorrow. You're both really under leveled. And, honestly, I want the raccoon to live. I can't dictate what is inside a lootbox, but I can choose the rarity sometimes... Anyway, if you live, you'll get a legendary box. If you kill something ten levels above you, I'll double it. This quest is shared between party members. Don't die. And don't let the raccoon die. I'll make your life hell if you do.

"Oh, that's interesting. I hadn't even thought about that," I said.

"Thought about what?"

"Where the lootboxes come from. They're just in games, and sometimes you get them from merchants or achievements. But *where* do they come from? I never put much thought into it."

It's too much to explain. It's not the Council, but it kinda is. And it's kinda like they come from the universe, but they don't. Gods can give lootboxes, though. Anyway, there's your explanation. They just exist.

"Well, there you go, Chris. Don't go questioning the laws

of the universe. You're clearly too dumb to understand it." Paco laughed.

I didn't comment, but he was right. The less I questioned how things worked, the better off I'd be, I felt. My whole life was a lie, and now I was living in the "true" universe, which was vastly different than anything I had ever known.

"Let's open our boxes," I said as I pulled the uncommon box first. It was made of iron, like the name said. There was a sigil where the keyhole should be. It was a white wolf with an ax behind it, dripping blood. The box opened. Inside, there was raw chicken, and a cloak.

Cloak of the Ranger

+2 Dexterity

"Alright, I guess I could use that." I opened the rare lootbox next.

Inside, there was more raw chicken, a wolf pelt, a few health potions, two thousand gold, and a quiver of arrows.

Arrows of the Dwarf Lord

These bad boys do double damage to the enemies of Lord Greatwood. Uncommon for a dwarf to use arrows, but much has changed since the great battle.

"Neat," I said as I equipped the cloak and took my arrows from my old quiver and added them to my new one. "What'd you get?" I asked Paco.

"I got some health potions, a full set of samurai armor, and another sword. But this one can't be upgraded. Oh, and I got two thousand gold."

He started equipping everything. Another sword sat on

his left hip, and his armor looked like classic samurai armor. It was colored red with gold trim.

"Holy shit," I muttered.

"It doesn't do much, just gives me buffs to Constitution and Strength. I wish it could be upgraded. But it says it can't."

"What're your stats now?"

"Uh, hold on, lemme use up my points," he said.

I pulled up my stats too, knowing he was going to ask me what they were.

Paco: here it's easier this way.

Strength: 12

Dexterity: 5

Constitution: 14

Intelligence: 4

Wisdom: 1

Charisma: 9

Chris: Mine are

Strength: 9

Dexterity: 16 (+2)

Constitution: 7

Intelligence: 2

Wisdom: 5

Charisma: 2

"That's not bad," Paco said. "Your dexterity is really good. We should get your Constitution and Charisma up when we can."

"Yeah, I wasn't focusing on them just yet. Your Constitution and Strength are really good so far. If we get your Intelligence up, maybe you can start using spells. But Dexterity would probably help you. Might turn into a ninja instead of a samurai," I chuckled.

"Ninjas are cool, but I don't want to throw things. I want to level up my sword."

"I wonder if there's a way to see what it levels up with. Hey, did you get any new abilities since you got another sword?" I asked.

"No. But I can dual-wield them. I don't know how my **Double Slash** ability works with both. Maybe each one activates, so it's like four hits?"

That is correct, raccoon. Each sword will now activate with an ability of your choosing.

"Oh, hell yeah!" Paco shouted as he stood up and unsheathed both of his swords, and started swinging them.

"Alright, Paco. I think we should head to the market and stock up on some supplies, then find that blacksmith and grab a piece of armor," I said as I stood up and began walking to the door.

"I don't know what kind of armor they could give me that I don't already have, but okay. Let's go," he hopped down off the couch. I half expected his samurai suit to clang around, but it didn't make too much noise.

We walked to the main square of the town. Everyone was out in full force today. The street was packed, which made for a claustrophobic amount of congestion. More than once we had to squeeze through a throng of dwarves. My cloak even got tangled up on a gentleman who was haggling for some mana potions, demanding that they be included with the price of whatever else he was purchasing.

"They're really angry today," Paco said.

"I think they're just anxious about tomorrow like we are. I don't blame them. It's war. Any of them might not come home."

"Why are they charging for supplies then? Doesn't the existence of this town rest on us winning?"

"It does, but I'm guessing some are going to stay back and defend the town. Besides, if they win, people make money, and money runs everything."

"It's a pretty stupid idea if you ask me."

"It is, but it isn't. Not everything can be free and exchanged on a barter system. And no one has the right to something someone else made."

"Yeah, but this is war. There should be a different set of rules."

"Remember what the AI said about our opinions on matters we have no place in?" I turned and faced Paco.

"I do. But this *is* our business now. I can have an opinion on this because *I'm* directly involved. Our lives are on the line, too. It's not like I have an opinion on faeries and doo-dads across the continent blowing themselves up over who owns what. I have an opinion on supplies to keep us alive because we were told we were going to fight in *their* war." Paco's voice was firm, and I understood his point. We were still getting free stuff, but he was clearly nervous that he might not make it back. The abduction was a fluke. The demon hawk we barely scraped by. Now we were seeing a real battle on a scale we couldn't comprehend because we had never been involved. Maybe if luck was on our side, the battle would be small and quick without much destruction. But, based on the quest the AI had given us, I highly doubted it would be easy.

"You're right. But we still gotta play by the rules. Who knows, maybe you can barter for a lower price. You do have Charisma higher than mine, and these people like you way more than they like me."

"Yeah, we'll see. I want to go look at the armor first, though. Then we can get supplies," he said as he waddled past me and beelined for the blacksmith.

The anvil hung above the door to the blacksmith. It was surprisingly clear in this section of town. There were only a few dwarves hanging around, and almost all of them were fully kitted out. They had menacing armor that covered every inch of their bodies except for their faces. Metal, which I assumed to be iron, hung down in between their eyes and covered their noses. Their mouths were free, and the beards flowed down to their chests. We walked into the blacksmith, and each of them went silent and nodded as we did.

"Ay, I been waitin' fer yuh two," a burly dwarf stood behind the counter. He was bald, but his beard was longer than any we had seen so far. It was braided from each end of his mustache and went down almost to his knees. "I'm Krostric Copperbasher."

"I'm Chris, and this is Paco."

"It's nice to meet you, Mr. Basher."

"I don't have much left fer ye. But I did put some stuff to

the side as Oakshoulder requested of me. Even made something for the little raccoon last night. Figured he would want something special. You on the other hand," he pointed to me, "I had to source some things, but got something you might want as well." He reached under the counter and placed pieces of armor for us to look at.

On the counter sat multiple helmets, a few pairs of iron boots, a piece of chainmail, and a full suit of iron armor, which did nothing but buff Constitution.

"What'd you make me?" Paco asked as he looked over the armor and saw nothing he wanted.

Krostric reached under the counter again and placed a mask for Paco to look at. It was made of some kind of metal, but it wasn't iron. It was entirely black, with two holes for Paco's eyes. Horns stood on the forehead, and a black rope hung from its teeth.

Mask of the Oni

+3 Strength

Ability to Threaten. Threatened enemies freeze in place for three seconds and take fifty percent more damage.

These monsters are feared in every culture. Enemies may cower as you run towards them. Bring hell with your blade and send your enemies back where they belong.

"That's it! I'll take it." Paco reached up to the counter and put on the mask. He turned to face me. He really looked menacing. The holes where his eyes were burned red.

"Holy shit," I muttered.

"And fer ye," Copperbasher reached down one last time, and produced a jacket.

It was plain brown leather with gold studs across the front.

Chest Piece of the Lone Ranger

+3 Constitution

Ability to Deflect. Incoming projectiles have a thirty percent chance to return to sender. Cooldown five minutes. Cool down doubles with each use until the end of the day.

Some say the Lone Ranger died heroically in battle; others say he wandered into the woods, choosing a life of peace when he took off his clothes and laid them down for someone else to take. Either way, this has been passed down through a lineage of archers and made its way to you. Cherish it, and pass it along when you no longer need it. That's what he would have wanted.

I grabbed it and equipped the item in my inventory. It was snug, but not overly so. I turned and twisted, figuring I'd feel the studs on my skin, but it was surprisingly nimble and not overbearing.

"I'll take it," I said.

"Ay, both are on the house. Paid for by Oakshoulder hisself. Anything else I can interest ye in will be full price."

"I think we need to go get supplies first, then come back if we need anything," I said. Paco nodded in agreement.

"Suit yerself. I'll be here, but I'm closing early. Be back before the sun gets two fingers close to the horizon. Gotta say goodnight to me wife and kids. If not, may Lord Greatwood bless ye and we fight side by side on the battlefield come tomorrow."

"May Lord Greatwood bless you," Paco said as he placed his arms at his sides and bowed. I nodded.

We both left the blacksmith and went to the center of town. The crowds were still bustling, but had cleared slightly. We weren't trying to push through dwarves anymore. Rather, we just waited in line until we could pass.

Paco found the first potion dealer he could and spent all of his gold on health. He had a measly fifty gold left when he was done, taking his total potions up to forty.

"Whatcha got?" I asked as I stepped up for my turn.

"Health potions are sixty-five gold each," the woman standing there said.

"Anything else?"

"Mana are the same. I also have defense potions for two hundred a piece, and strength for two hundred."

I looked over to inspect them. The strength potions gave plus-ten for a thirtyminute period. The defense potions gave a buff that eliminated twenty percent of damage done for ten-minute intervals. Both were really viable options. I had ten health potions, but I knew I wanted at least one of each of those.

"I'll take one defense, one strength—

"I want a strength potion!" Paco shouted. "Chris, take my gold." He immediately pulled out his fifty gold and handed it to me.

"Make that two strength potions, and I'll take twenty-two health potions."

It brought me up to thirty-two, which I figured would be enough.

"Here," I said as I tossed Paco a strength potion. I knew with the buff from his mask, taking the potion would bring him up to twenty-five Strength, and that would be formidable to say the least with his abilities and dual sword combo.

"What do we have left in gold?" he asked.

"Twenty. Not enough to go back to the blacksmith and get anything."

"Maybe you can get some supplies for food and cook up something. You have all that chicken."

I thought about it for a moment before I turned back to the woman.

"You got any recipes or food for sale? Anything that would give us some buffs?"

"Sorry, hun. Not my specialty. The market is also closed now with the sun setting; otherwise, I'd send you over to the butcher."

I turned back to Paco, made a face, and shook my head.

"Guess we should go home then," he said as he turned and started weaving between the legs of all the dwarves who were heading home.

I tried to keep up with him, but he beat me back to the house. He was sitting on the couch finishing his coleslaw by the time I walked in. His oni mask sat on the table, but he still donned all of his armor.

"We should come up with a plan," I said as I sat across from him.

He chewed silently and stared into the empty fireplace.

"I want to complete that quest and get double rewards," Paco said between bites.

"That means we need to kill something that's at least level 19. We're about to level up, and I think once the fighting starts, we'll get XP pretty quickly."

"So, then we find something that's level 19 and kill it."

"I really would rather stay near the mage and have the protection."

"But, the loot. Double rewards when we live."

If, I thought to myself.

"If we time it right, I can threaten someone, then double slash them while you use deadeye. It'll work. My strength will be buffed to twenty-five, and yours will be at nineteen. You'll do double damage with those new arrows if goblins are enemies of Lord Greatwood, too."

"You've clearly been thinking about this."

"Of course I have! I want that treasure, Chris."

"Tomorrow, before the fight, let's talk to Brukrag and ask him if goblins would take double damage, just to be sure."

"We're going to do it," Paco said as he placed his bowl down and picked up his oni mask. "They're going to fear us." He placed the mask back on. The eyes started to burn red again. Paco turned away and went to his manhole cover without uttering another word.

I lay in bed tossing and turning. Thinking about my life and what it had become. The nervousness about what was about to happen was getting the best of me, and I still didn't know what this war would look like. I knew the mech would be on our side, and we'd have a shield from a mage, but other than that, what could I expect except the complete unknown?

CHAPTER 15

BRUKRAG WAS WAITING outside our house before the sun even came out. The sky was clear, and the stars were bright, but no moon hung there watching over us.

"Good morning," he said after knocking on our door. His fists rumbled the entire house, so much so that Paco and I both thought there was an earthquake. We jumped out of bed and ran for the door, thinking the walls would come crashing down at any moment.

"Good morning, Mr. Shoulder," Paco said as he fumbled with his gear and eventually put on his oni mask.

"I see you both got your armor for the upcoming battle."

"We did," I said. "But I had a question about something I received in a lootbox." I showed Brukrag the arrows I had received.

"By the gods!" His eyes were wide with astonishment. I placed one of the arrows in his hands, which he closely inspected. His eyes came so close to the point of the arrow that I feared he might stab himself and accidentally go blind.

"Are goblins considered enemies of Lord Greatwood?" I asked.

"Ay. They are. And you said you received these from a lootbox?"

"I did. Why?"

"We haven't seen this craftsmanship in centuries. The magic to make these has long been forgotten by our culture. May I keep one for further study? I do not own one myself."

"Of course," I said as I put my quiver on my back minus one arrow.

"Good," Brukrag said as he put the arrow into his inventory. "Come, it is time for the march to the southern plane." He turned, and we followed back towards the starport. We continued past it and to a line of trees, which were much darker than the hues of pink I had become accustomed to.

"Where is everyone else?" Paco asked as we made our way through the treeline.

"They left late last night and set up camp while you two were sleeping. Our vanguard is ready at the far edge of this tree line. Just before the sun peaks over the horizon, we will begin our assault on Squish the Goblin King and his city."

"They seem to live pretty close to you guys," I said.

"That they do, but we have lived in peace for a while. The baby demon hawk incident has caused our truce to be void. Now we may rid this land of the vermin who are not our peers." Brukrag's voice was thick with hatred. I didn't know what had caused the truce, why it existed in the first place considering how much he hated the goblins, but it seemed that our intrusion surely helped deteriorate a treaty he did not want in the first place.

We walked for maybe another half hour between the trees, mostly in silence. There were hundreds of dwarves waiting in the darkness when he finally met up with them. Brukrag took us further down the line until we met up with a dwarven mage.

"This is Brukhun Goldvoice," Brukrag said as he introduced us. The dwarf was about the same build as Brukrag, but his hair was ghostly white. His beard hung from his mustache and was braided with fine golden tinsel running through it. On his back rested a gold-headed ax, and a wooden staff with a blackish-blue orb at the top.

"Nice to finally meet you two. I've been busy working with my nephew here as of late on important matters." He put out his hand. Paco graciously accepted. I did the same. His grip almost broke every bone in my hand as I felt them shift.

"Nice to meet you, too," I said as I rubbed my hand to ease the soreness that had already set into it.

"You'll be with me the majority of this battle. I will have a protection spell going to stop the trebuchets. Should any goblins breach my shield, feel free to slay them without mercy. Your arrows will be allowed to shoot out from the barrier," he said before I could even question him.

"Will we be fighting in the city, too?" Paco asked.

"I do not believe so. But we shall see what the day brings. Brukrag will pilot his mech with the vanguard, and we will give him backup from just beyond this tree line. When he gets to Squish and the goblin king falls, the city will be ours. The other goblins will indeed flee, most likely to the mountains. That is where the golems and dragons live," Brukhun replied.

"Do you think they'll team up with the golems or dragons for a counter-attack?" I asked.

"Doubtful. Dragons do not concern themselves with the politics of goblins, nor dwarves. They think themselves too high-blood to bother," Brukhun was firm.

"Interesting," I muttered.

"Thank you, Brukhun," Brukrag said. "But I must go and ready the final preparations."

"May Lord Greatwood bless you this fine day," Brukhun slapped his hand on Brukrag's shoulder as they put their foreheads together.

"By the ax of Lord Greatwood, may our swords never dull and our shields never splinter. With his fury, may the ground we walk upon give way to dust and rubble. With his patience, may the waves still and the winds fall silent in our presence. With his mercy, may our souls find peace within the earth we once emerged. Lord Greatwood, guide my hand. I am Brukrag, your humble vassal, come to this land to do thy bidding until I am once again called home. Hoy."

I watched as Brukrag departed and left us with the dwarf mage. Finally, I was able to notice those around us. Most of the other dwarves held axes, while some carried bows, and a few had spears. There was one other mage who wore all green and had a pitch-black beard laced with green tinsel.

"Who is that?" I asked as I pointed to the other mage.

"That is my brother, Brukward. Ever the youngest brother. He will command the attack spells while I defend. He does not talk much."

Brukward looked over at us and caught my eye. He did not wave, only nodded his head before turning with his hands behind his back. He stared far off into the distance toward the edge of the tree line.

We stood there with Brukhun for what felt like an eternity of silence. I noticed Paco shivering. It was oddly cold, but I felt like it wasn't from the weather, but rather his nerves getting to him. I felt antsy, and the same tremor went down my arms and legs as adrenaline started to course through my body from the anticipation.

"Eyes up," Brukhun said.

To our right, we saw the mech light up with an ethereal green glow. The ground beneath us started to shake as it took its first steps, crashing through the trees. They splintered and came thudding to the ground.

"Follow me," Brukhun's voice boomed as the vanguard started shouting as they ran for the clearing.

We walked with Brukhun through the brush until we came to the edge. In front of us, we could see an open landscape. The ground was blackened, and no vegetation grew. On the horizon, we saw the goblin city. The buildings were made out of sheet metal, it looked like. It reminded me of playing one map from the old PvP shooter in the early 2000s. There were no windows, just stacks of metal boxes on top of each other. It looked like any one of them could come crashing down if the wind blew hard enough.

At the base of the city, a wall blockaded anyone from entering, though it, too, was made of the same metal.

"It looks flimsy, the entire city, I mean."

"Trust me, Chris. Though goblins scavenge and jerry-rig everything together, that does not mean what they make is easily destroyed. They know how to enhance and buff their fortifications. Though they may seem dull, they are masters of their craft, albeit a little haphazard and quick."

I looked down at Paco, who was now watching the dwarves cross the open field. Brukrag's mech was still leading the charge. Deep sirens blared from the goblin city, like someone blowing a battle horn. Lights flickered on and illuminated the last of the night sky as the sun peaked over the horizon.

"Get down!" Brukhun shouted as he grabbed his staff and spread his arms out wide. I watched a blue dome cover us as a flaming red orb launched from the city in our direction. It came down early and landed maybe a football field in front of us, shattering on impact. Each chunk of the rock spread out, glowed red, then exploded in a rain of molten earth. I watched as the vanguard of dwarves ahead dove away from the impact and successive explosions. Some were not as lucky as others.

"Move up with me," Brukhun said. He stepped forward, and the shield around us moved with him. As long as we stayed close by, we would be safe—I hoped. My chest was tight, and my heart was racing from the first trebuchet.

"Chris, I'm scared," Paco said as I felt his armor bump up against my leg.

"Me too," I whispered. "Just stay close to Brukhun."

More flaming rocks from trebuchets started flying through the air, and I could see demon hawks with goblins on their backs circling the city. Brukrag's mech started to swing wildly in front of itself now. I heard a muttering to my left and turned to see Brukward praying into his hands. He made a quick motion, then lifted his hand to the sky. Earth moved in front of him, congealed itself into a ball, and turned green before he punched it. The projectile shot wildly fast across the battlefield and towards one of the goblin trebuchet projectiles. It collided head-on and showered the landscape below with more explosions.

"Holy shit," I said. "Why are they exploding after a delay?" I turned to Brukhun who had started to move forward again.

"Those bastards imbue their projectiles with explosives and magic. Each fragment probably has a goblin boomstick attached to it that activates afte—get down!"

Before I could turn back to see what Brukhun shouted about, I felt my world ripple. We had taken a direct hit from a trebuchet. The impact caused the shield to flicker out of existence, then back in front of us before the secondary explosions. My ears rang. Paco was on the ground next to me, his face in the dirt. I quickly bent down and lifted him to his feet.

"Are you okay?" I shouted so loud I could barely hear my own voice from the ringing in my ears.

"I don't want to be here, Chris." There was fear in Paco's voice underneath his oni mask. "We're going to die."

"No, you are not, little one. Stay within the shield. Do not distract me with any more questions. Focus on moving forward and listen to what I say. The shield will protect you."

"It barely protected us from that!" Paco shouted back.

Brukhun shot a look at Paco. "Lord Greatwood provides and protects. By his blood, I will keep you alive even if it is the last thing I do before going to Valhalla. Now move!" Brukhun stomped forward. I followed with Paco clinging to my side.

The battle in front of us was now in full swing. The gates to the goblin city had opened, and a tsunami of bodies had poured out. Dwarves hacked and slashed as they met their enemy head-on. Behind us, waves of arrows came from the treeline. They arced over and continued toward friend and foe alike.

We marched forward again. I watched as Brukward continued to hurl green orbs at the projectiles in the sky. We had almost reached the first hole in the ground when I saw him. The first dwarf to die.

His legs were gone, and his intestines hung from his stomach. There were large holes where molten rock ripped through him. His skin was pale, and his pupils were wide. I doubled over and threw up.

"Get up and move!" Brukhun's voice pierced the trauma I had just witnessed. The ringing in my ears was starting to subside, and I wished it hadn't.

Around me, I heard yelling, but then something else was cutting through the air. Crying. Pleading coming from other dwarves. Many called for their mothers, fathers, or for Lord Greatwood to take away their pain before guiding them into

Valhalla. The horror of war was truly setting in as more and more projectiles were raining down on everyone. I scanned in front of us. Brukrag's mech was still up and running. That gave me hope. Very little, but it loosened the knot in my chest by one percent. Maybe.

CHAPTER 16

WE CREPT SLOWLY to the middle of the battlefield as the war raged on in front of us. I was still feeling the shell shock of the trebuchet that collided with our shield, but Brukward was taking them out faster and faster now as more projectiles lit up the sky. Blood pooled in the war-torn landscape, and more than once did we step into one of those craters filled with blood and gore while listening to the screams of our comrades.

"Hold!" Brukhun shouted as he came to a halt.

"What is it?" Paco asked.

"I dunno. Something ain't right." He stared towards the city. Brukrag had made little progress, and the goblin swarm kept coming from the walls of the city. There had to be at least fifty thousand of them. I watched as tiny explosions appeared in the dwarf vanguard. I assumed it was from the goblin boomsticks Brukhun had warned us about.

"Do you feel that?" Paco looked up at me.

"Feel what?" I asked.

"The ground is rumbling."

"Retreat! Everyone retreat!" Brukhun shouted to his left and right as he waved his staff. A projection of himself appeared in the sky above everyone. "Brothers, fall back!"

Brukhun turned to us and aimed his staff. A blue beam shot out at us. "Run. It won't do much against a direct hit from a trebuchet, but it will protect you. Get out of here —now!"

I didn't question it; all I saw was a newly formed shield around us, which was not nearly as vast as the moving fortress he had cast earlier.

"Let's go," I said to Paco as we turned and ran back for the tree line.

The ground really started to rumble then. Paco had noticed it, but no one else had. Now it felt like the ground was literally moving beneath our feet. Behind us, I heard screams, crashing, and the world ending. I turned to take a look.

A pit had opened up, and a monstrosity of a goblin crawled out. He had to be at least forty feet tall, if not more. He wore a red robe covered in jewels. Across his arms and shoulders were gold bands. His fingers were coated with so many rings that I could barely see his skin. He brandished a golden sword. I watched as Brukrag's mech ran over to him. It was slightly more than half his height.

"Shit," I muttered as my overlay inspected him.

Squish the Goblin King: Level 35

Watch out for this bastard. He takes more than he gives. Rules with a golden fist. Each of those rings was stolen throughout the years from some great lord or lady. And don't touch his pigs. He loves those pigs.

"What pigs?" I said aloud as I stood in awe and horror of the goblin king.

"Those pigs," Paco pointed.

I squinted and saw five pigs attached to Squish's feet.

Squish's Five Little Piggies: Level 1

They're cute. They're lovable. They eat the remains of Squish's enemies. They hate the goblin king, but what can they do? He experimented a long time ago on his favorite pig to make copies of him. The spell backfired, and the pigs replaced his toes. It took some getting used to, but he was happy with the outcome even though he learned he shouldn't use magic. Now, Squish uses his piggies to stomp his enemies in a sick, sadistic ritual of honoring his favorite pet.

"What the fuck?" I said with my mouth agape.

Squish had crawled out of the hole he created in the ground and was now wreaking havoc on the dwarven army. With each stomp, I watched as dwarves scattered or exploded in a shower of gore that coated the green skin of his feet in a crimson. He laughed maniacally each time he succeeded.

"Quit standing there and run!" Brukhun's voice broke through the violence.

I turned my head and saw the mage standing there waving his staff. In front of him, shields appeared on others in the army. Paco grabbed the sleeve of my shirt and tugged on it.

"Chris, we have to do something," he said as his oni mask stared back at me.

"What can we do about that?" I pointed.

"I don't know, but we can't leave Brukrag to fight Squish all by himself. We *have* to find a way to help."

I hated it. The thought of running towards our certain death, but he was right. We had no place to go if Brukrag lost, unless the grays came back to pick us up. And by then, who knew what would happen? We were both terrified and traumatized from the battle already, but we needed to help, no matter how minor it was. I nodded to Paco.

"Let's go."

I pulled my bow out and started grabbing arrows from my quiver. We ran forward towards Brukhun. He watched us as we breached the far side of his shield and headed towards the madness.

"You fools!" he shouted. "Brukward, give them covering fire!" I heard from behind us.

As we ran, I saw fresh green masses of earth come crashing down further in front of us into the horde of goblins. Brukward was now worrying about giving us a clear path to Squish rather than the projectiles from the trebuchets. I thought it was a stupid idea. At least me and Paco could fight through the goblins—even if we sucked at it. I still welcomed the offensive protection either way.

We reached the rear of Brukrag's vanguard and came to a stop. We scanned the battlefield looking for his mech. He was off to our right, fighting through a throng of goblins, trying to make his way to Squish.

"Let's meet up with Brukrag, then we worry about the goblin king," I said to Paco. He nodded and turned. I watched as he pulled his **Lackluster Sword** out and ran forward. His blade cut through the wind.

"Has he gotten faster?" I muttered as I tried to keep pace with him.

I started shooting arrows towards the crowd, where mostly goblins or slain dwarves were. I still wasn't confident in my aim, even though I had gotten better. I did not want to shoot a comrade accidentally in the back with one of my arrows. My arrows flew, and I saw my experience bar slowly tick up. I don't know what I killed, but I got an achievement that I quickly ignored.

We pushed our way to the front of the fighting. I pulled my dagger and put my bow on my back as I watched Paco slice goblins across the chest and throat. More than once he hacked off a green limb that fell with a sickening plop to the ground below. He spun and moved in ways that I'd only seen in action movies that were comically bad. But he was effective. I tried to stand back from much of the direct fighting, only stabbing two goblins in the back while they fought and lashed out at a dwarf in front of them.

"This isn't going to work," I said despairingly. Paco was starting to get closer to Brukrag's mech and deeper into the fray. I put my dagger away and looked around. On the ground were flimsy, rusted swords dropped by dead goblins, which looked more like they'd give you a nasty tetanus infection rather than cut through dwarven armor.

I kept my eye on Paco and surveyed the ground, trying to stick close to the midline of the dwarves.

"Oy! Ranger, get to the back!" someone shouted.

"I'm with him!" I pointed to Paco. He was now fighting two or three goblins at a time.

"Take this then and go help!" the dwarf shouted as he threw his ax. I clumsily caught it. The ax was lighter than it appeared.

Dwarven Ax

Hack and slash. Rip me from their skulls. Pulverize their bones under your feet.

Strength +1

"That'll do," I said as I ran through the midline to catch up with Paco. There were a few dwarves around him. They had created a semicircle and slowly started marching forward towards Brukrag. He had become separated from the army. I watched as he swung the giant ax and punched down on any goblin in front of him.

"Paco, I'm here!" I yelled as I caught up to him and slammed the ax into the head of a goblin who was coming up behind him. Its body immediately went limp, and when I put my foot on the back of its neck to pull the ax out, its limbs jerked.

"Where'd you get that?" Paco asked.

"Someone back there gave it to me."

"I'll trade you my other sword for it," his red eyes burned into me.

"Not a chance." My heart was racing now. My XP had gone up, and I had received another achievement. Something had clicked in both of us, I could tell. Maybe it was that we weren't having flaming explosives lobbed at us anymore, or something primal had kicked in. But we were here, and we were fighting. We'd deal with the consequences to our mental state after. All we had to do now was get to Brukrag with the six or seven dwarves who stood next to us.

CHAPTER 17

THE WALL of dwarves made their push forward to Brukrag who was slowly cutting his way across the battlefield as Squish gleefully cheered and stomped on anyone around him. I watched as dwarves and goblins suffered the same fate. Destroyed by piggies.

"Squish must squish!" his high-pitched voice reverberated around us.

I pulled arrows from my quiver and started shooting any goblin who came towards our front line, making sure to pull the arrows from their lifeless corpses when we marched over them. Paco was among those standing with the dwarves as they hacked their way through.

Behind us, I could see Brukward and Brukhun casting shields and shooting flaming projectiles that came too close to them. They would then send a volley of mortars back towards the goblin city, which was quickly followed by a stream of arrows that could almost block out the sun. I don't remember seeing many dwarven archers, but there had to be a reinforcement that came through, unless Brukward had conjured arrow magic. The thought crossed my mind, and it seemed reasonable enough. I had seen it in plenty of RPGs before. A spellcaster rained down arrows on a specific area of the battlefield while they went about their lives. I wondered and hoped I'd be able to learn that ability one day.

"Brace!" One of the dwarves in front of me shouted as a new wave of goblins came crashing from the city gate. They were holding wooden shields and wore comically large helmets, which had bloodied spikes on the front. I watched as they ran towards us, their helmets bobbing and turning, so they'd have to stop and readjust them. A few had thrown them to the ground, while some others face-planted in the dirt, which had turned to mud from the pooling of blood.

The dwarves pressed closer together. One in the center, whose name I did not get, started chanting. It sounded like complete gibberish you'd read in an H.P. Lovecraft story mixed with a Gregorian chant. A series of blue magical shields appeared before them and interlocked across the entire semicircle. Goblins crashed into them with clangs and bangs as the dwarves hacked their axes down over the shields. Red blood spewed in arcs as they pulled bloodied heads from the bodies trying to break the formation. Paco had jumped atop the chanting dwarf and stabbed his sword downward. Each time it came back bloodier than the last. I closed the small distance on the left and joined the formation as I equipped my new ax.

Goblins came faster as I did so. I had beheaded one with a quick side-swipe and almost hit the shields protecting us.

"Watch where yer swingin' that thing!" one of them shouted at me.

"Sorry," I said meekly as I changed my stance to allow for a better overhand swing. It was a learning curve to use a bow, but my class made it easier. Though I understood how to use an ax in theory, each swing of it made me feel off balance. Either it was because of my class, or I really was that stupid and didn't understand my own center of gravity.

I noticed my level had gone up to 11 when I looked at our party. He had already hit level 13. How? I had no clue. We shared experience to an extent, and he hadn't killed many more goblins than me. At least, I didn't think he did. I looked over at him. His oni mask made him emotionless. He was simply killing or maiming anyone who came near him. Underneath it though, I believed he was sweating bullets. His swings and stabs were erratic, and he was losing control of himself in the horrors of this war. Each goblin that came up on a side he wasn't watching made him jerk and swing in a way that seemed more foreign than his samurai skills let on. As I watched him, I noticed something peculiar. His sword seemed different, longer, its color more vibrant. The lone green leaf seemed richer than usual. The handle looked as if there was a black band of cloth now wrapped around it. I wondered if it had leveled up again.

We pushed through the swarm and found ourselves fighting within ten feet of Brukrag.

"Brothers! I am honored to have you fight by my side once

again. Lord Greatwood blesses us," a robotic monotone voice boomed from the mech.

"It is nice to be by your side again, nephew," the dwarf who cast the shield spell boomed as he swung his ax and split a goblin in half. Its intestines flopped around as I looked and saw the inside of its body covered in the same red gore I was becoming desensitized to.

"We must get over to Squish," Brukrag said. "Brukstorm, do you think you can help with that?"

"Yes, nephew. Quickly. Everyone surround me and fight as if your lives depended on it."

I watched as Brukstorm took a step back from the center line and the dwarves made a tight, complete circle around him. Paco stood next to me, and we in turn were the closest to Brukrag's mech. There was heat coming off of it that was almost intolerable. I felt myself starting to sweat more. Another Gregorian-Cthulu-esqe chant rumbled behind me.

My ax swung more easily as time went on. The chanting continued for what felt like an hour. The battle was raging on so long that the sun was now at its highest in the sky. When I could, I watched Brukrag's mech make huge sweeping cuts across the battlefield, completely obliterating any goblin that came close. Still, the hordes kept on coming, and I wondered where all these goblins were coming from. The archers, Brukward, and Brukhun were doing their best with the demon hawks and goblins in the sky who dropped explosives down, but the projectiles from the trebuchets were starting to land on the battlefield now. The screams and cries of dwarves were now becoming commonplace. Inescapable even.

I watched as the sky grew dark. A series of black and green clouds rolled through as the wind picked up. Rain began pelting us, and it was harder to see Brukrag's mech ten feet away. I knew it was there only because of the ethereal glow. The goblins that attacked us dwindled, probably from the poor visibility. The explosions from the trebuchets continued, but the demon hawks and their captains completely disappeared. I turned and looked at Brukstorm. He was glowing. A black aura emanated fromhim, and his eyes were a solid neon green. His mouth was agape and did not move, but the chanting still came from his lungs. The storm clouds stopped, and the rain bore down as hard as I had ever seen it in my life. Then, in an instant, everything was chaos.

The rain had stopped immediately, and I saw a funnel in the center of the clouds. It was directly above Squish. From the eye of the storm came a large flaming meteor. Squish looked up and laughed maniacally, like a deranged clown. I watched as he took his sword, and just when the meteor was about to hit, he swung and connected with it. The meteor launched like a baseball through the atmosphere. It had ripped massive holes in the clouds, at least two hundred feet wide. Just as I felt the sweltering heat from it, it had dispersed in an instant.

"Fools! Your dwarven magic does not work on me!" He raised his sword and pointed it directly at Brukrag.

While I had direct sight of him, I quickly used **Scan.**

Squish, Goblin King. Level 35

Immune to dwarven magic

Immune to dwarven weapons

Blessed by

"Shit. He's immune!" I shouted.

"What?" Brukrag's voice boomed.

"I scanned him, and it says he's immune to dwarven weapons and magic. It says 'blessed by' someone. It's just a black box."

"Quick, Chris, Paco, to me!"

Brukrag's mech bent down, and his hand opened. Paco and I climbed onto it.

"Retreat!" he shouted as the dwarves that surrounded us climbed onto the back of the mech.

Brukrag's mech carried us as he started running for the tree line. Squish cackled in the background.

"Nephew, please. Stop," Brukstorm said. Brukrag came to a halt and turned. "It's time. For Lord Greatwood."

"Uncle, this is foolish."

"You knew it would be from the start. Ready the cannon!"

There was no reply from Brukrag, but a humming sound

came from the mech as the cannons on its shoulders moved. I watched as dwarves lined up and placed themselves in the tubes.

"No fucking way," I whispered.

"For Lord Greatwood!" an echoing shout came from the tubes in unison as a blast ripped through my eardrums. I watched as the dwarves came shooting out with their axes drawn. They launched across the battlefield directly at Squish. He stumbled as he was hit by the dwarves.

"My eye! My fucking eye!"

A health bar finally appeared above Squish's head. He had taken damage.

"It worked!" Paco shouted.

"He's immune to dwarven magic and weapons, but he's not immune to dwarves," Brukrag muttered.

"Ready the cannon!" The next round of dwarves shouted as they opened the back hatch and loaded themselves into it.

"For Lord Greatwood!" The shouts came again as the cacophonous explosion made me go deaf.

I watched in horror as the dwarves shot themselves out of the cannon atop the shoulder of the wooden mech. Each came flying out with astounding speed and impaled themselves onto Squish.

A notification popped up.

Trade Requested from Brukrag Oakshoulder. Do you accept?

I hit "Yes."

Immediately four potions popped up, and I accepted without giving anything in return.

"What's this?"

"The night will be long. I have given you and Paco what potions I have. May they keep you safe."

I inspected the new item in my inventory.

Blessing of Lord Greatwood.

Drink this before taking damage. If life-ending damage occurs, you will be left with 1HP. Just enough to cash in on your spells or a regular healing potion. If life-ending damage does not occur, fifty percent reduction in damage from enemies of Lord Greatwood.

"Why are you giving this to us?"

"Soon, you will have to fend for yourself. I fear this battle will not go as expected. May Lord Greatwood give you strength," Brukrag said as he set us down on the battlefield. "I must go. The cannons have fired, and soon my army will be on me ready to sacrifice their lives to stop this goblin menace."

"Brukrag, don't go!" Paco shouted. "We can regroup and figure something out. No one else needs to kill themselves to do damage to him."

"Little one, I fear that is not the case." Brukrag's mech bent down, and Brukrag went eye to eye with Paco.

Paco looked at me. I nodded, knowing what he was thinking.

CHAPTER 18

"GET OUT OF THE CANNONS!" Brukrag shouted as me and Paco hopped onto the mech and stuffed ourselves in.

"No. Now aim at Squish and send us on our way!" Paco shouted from the tube over.

"You'll die when you hit him," Brukrag said.

Paco and I had already drunk a potion and knew this was going to hurt—a lot.

"Not with these potions. Besides, Chris and I are the only ones here who aren't using dwarven weapons. We can hurt him!"

"He's too powerful. You won't be able to."

"Do you remember what the description of Squish said?" Paco asked.

"We all do. Why?" Brukrag said.

"I'm going to kill the pigs," Paco's voice was stern.

"You're mad. That'll just make him angrier," Brukrag replied.

"But he loves the pigs, and we can hurt them. That'll be enough time to distract him and figure something out. Now aim the cannons and fire!" Paco's voice reverberated through the long metal tubes.

I looked from where I had stuffed myself. Down the long metal pipe, there was little light as Brukrag had turned towards the ground. Slowly, the mech stood up and turned. I could see nothing but light shining through. I used my hand to block it.

"May Lord Greatwood bless you this fine day and may you be greeted at the gates of Valhalla with open arms," Brukrag's robotic voice said.

I felt the hum of power before I had my eardrums completely eradicated from my skull. The force pressed against me, and I felt my ribs break. I hit a regular potion and brought my health back to full as I saw the ground beneath us. I then used another of Brukrag's potions in case the effect from the launch had cancelled out the protection. As the wind whipped my hair and stung my eyes, I tried to focus on Squish.

We soared through the air at such a high rate of speed; I thought I was about to shit out my heart. I pulled my dagger in my right hand and held it in front of me as Squish's face became bigger and bigger.

My arms broke as I collided with the goblin king. My spine felt like it was going to rip through my stomach, and I'd be separated from my own skin. The world went dark as I splayed out on the goblin king. My health bar was at a pixel as it flashed red. I hit a health potion as the world started going dark. The readjustment of my bones and regrowth of my muscles was something I'd never get used to.

"Chris! It hurts. It hurts so bad," Paco's voice came from my right. I looked over and saw him hanging from his sword. It had completely impaled itself in Squish's eye. Blood ran down Squish's face and covered Paco's already crimson armor.

The world was coming back into view as I hung there with Paco. I had a death grip on my small knife, while Paco hung from the rope that was attached to his sword. I watched as his arm moved unnaturally back into its socket. He moaned the entire time his bones reset themselves.

Squish was flailing and screaming about his eyes. I looked down. Under his feet, goblins and dwarves were getting crushed. His green feet were a smear of intestines and bones. The little piggies he had for toes were trying to eat whatever body parts they could as they came crashing back down to the battlefield.

"Paco, we need to get down!" I shouted.

"Jump?" he yelled across.

"I think we should try to land on his clothing; we can do some damage on the way down," I said as I looked down at the garb underneath his golden armor. It was tattered, but I felt like we could grab it if we timed everything correctly.

Paco nodded, then grabbed Squish's eyelid. He ripped his sword out, stuck it in the sheath, and dropped before I could say anything.

Squish squealed with pain.

"Shit," I said as I pulled an arrow from my quiver, jammed it into Squish's skin, and pulled the knife out. I dropped and aimed as best I could for the flowing, tattered red cloth beneath his ocean of gold.

I felt myself bounce off his armor and crash to the ground. I was on my back staring at the sky. Squish was stomping around, and I knew I needed to get up. I used another health potion and hopped to my feet. Lightning bolts shot through my back and my legs.

"Chris! Get the pigs!" Paco's voice sounded distant through the clanging of armor and crashing of footfalls. I mashed down on another health potion.

I watched my health bar slowly creep back to the green as I stood up and produced my bow. I aimed at one of the five little piggies on Squish's right foot. I knocked an arrow and let it fly at the largest one. It connected with the soft belly. The pig squealed and tried to bite the arrow sticking out of it. Warm blood dripped down. Squish's health bar had dropped from the arrow to the pig.

"My piggies!" he screamed and stomped down harder. I jumped back as his foot came down in front of me. The shockwave and rumble of the earth made me feel like I was about to lose my balance.

The pig continued to squeal, and I felt horrible about it. None of them wanted to be a part of Squish and his temper tantrum. It was just a science experiment gone wrong.

"Paco, change of plans. Cut the pigs loose!" I shouted. I looked over to see Paco in his samurai armor slashing at goblins in his way as he tried to carve a path over to me. I looked back at Squish's foot and finally got a closer look.

The pigs were attached where his toes were. They still had all of their legs, but where their ass should have been, that part connected to Squish. There was a clear distinction between his green skin and the pink or spotted colors of the pigs. It reminded me of that movie where the psychopath sewed people's mouths to someone's ass. The name eluded me.

I hoped my plan would work when Paco cut the pigs free. We could heal them if nothing detrimental was destroyed. Then maybe, just maybe, the pigs would help us fight Squish. I remembered their description. They loathed the goblin king. Hopefully, more than they hated us for hurting them.

Paco cartwheeled through the air and came down hard on the largest pig. His blade went right through it, but he misjudged the angle. The pig was cut in half. Its organs spilled out onto the ground. Its eyes were lifeless just as quickly as Paco had done it.

"Not like that! Cut them where they attach to Squish!" I pulled an arrow and shot directly up at the goblin king as he howled in pain. My arrow struck him in the hand, but did barely any damage. He lifted his foot and started to rub the spot where the largest pig had been.

"You'll pay for this!" he screeched as he stomped down. Paco dove toward me as I watched Squish ready his sword. His health bar had decreased a good five percent after the largest pig was killed.

Paco started slashing at the pigs, cutting the other four

free from Squish's foot. I ran over, shooting arrows at any goblin that ran towards the commotion we had created.

"Heal them!" I shouted at Paco, who had just freed the littlest pig from his prison. Paco started pulling health potions from his inventory and dosing the pigs with them. I watched as their health bars slowly regenerated and the red skulls marking them as enemies turned white to non-hostile.

I turned away from Paco and continued to shoot arrows at goblins running towards us brandishing their rusty swords. My quiver started to get low as the swarm focused their attention on us.

"Paco, we're going to have a problem here!" I shouted over my shoulder.

"I'm coming! The pigs are biting Squish!"

I turned to see the pigs grouped together. They were running after whatever foot they could get to. The goblin king was now missing chunks out of his good foot, while his toeless foot was pouring blood where his pigs used to be.

Paco popped up beside me and started throwing his sword at the incoming goblins. I watched as it soared through the air and pierced through their heads. Paco would then pull back on the cord attached to his hip and rip the sword back through their skulls as they collapsed to the ground.

"Cover me," I said. "I need to get some arrows back." I ran toward the closest goblins I had slain and started pulling my arrows back from their skulls with a sickening gurgle. One word stuck in my head as I did it. *Cartilaginous.* My quiver was finally feeling heavy again.

"Friends! I have returned," Brukrag's mech boomed

across the battlefield. I turned to see him running towards us. The pigs were keeping Squish busy as he hopped around trying to stop their biting. His health had fallen below half because of them. I saw their levels had increased to three across the board. They had grown larger, except the one that was where his pinky toe should have been—that one had stayed the same size but was leveling up all the same.

CHAPTER 19

BRUKRAG HAD MADE it across the battlefield. He swung the mech's arms and sent goblins soaring left and right as he did so. Squish had been pushed back about a football field away towards the gate of his city. Paco and I had finally found our groove now that we weren't dodging Squish's feet while Brukward and Brukhun focused on the trebuchets.

There was a blue name in our party now, but it was generically named "Pet." I didn't focus too hard or think too long about it. When the fighting was done—if we survived—I'd figure it out. Or my AI would tell me all about it; I was sure of that.

There was a large crashing sound. I looked to my right and saw Squish had fallen into the gate of his city. His health bar was blinking red. There was a large wooden spike through his chest where the city wall had slammed through him.

"Oh my God, they're doing it!" I shouted.

Brukrag's mech wasn't far off. "No, Chris. You did it. You crazy bastards. You actually did it," the mechanoid voice resounded through the air as his arms swung left and right like a child having too much fun in an excavator. With each rotation, goblins went flying. More than once, I could have sworn I saw a dwarf in the mix, clearly dead as his body rag dolled through the air.

"Chris, I want his loot!" Paco shouted. I turned to see him running through the throng of bodies towards Squish.

"Fucking hell," I muttered. I put my bow away and pulled the ax back out of my inventory as I ran as hard as I could towards Paco and the broken gate.

The goblins were slowing down now, with very few coming to the battle. More than once, I watched as groups of goblins threw their weapons to the ground and begged for mercy as they surrendered. Unfortunately for them, I quickly found out the dwarves did not accept surrender. They were executed on the spot with either a sharp ax or the dull thunk of a hammer. Others simply ran away from the battlefield towards the far-off mountains.

Paco was stabbing Squish in the legs when I caught up to him. His high-pitched screeching was getting worse, and I knew the end was near without even looking at his health bar. The pigs had grown to level 10. All except one had turned into a hulking boar with massive tusks and a hairy body. The other was the littlest pig. It was still plump, pink with splotches of black skin, and a tuft of white hair on its head that looked like a slicked-down mohawk. Above the pig, the word "pet" was illuminated in blue.

"Huh," I said. "That's interesting."

I swung the ax at any goblin that came near, but very few came to Squish's aid. I once again pulled my bow and loosed non-enchanted arrows at his face. They struck his eyes. When his health got to a pixel, I smashed down on my **Deadeye**. The final arrow went from my bow with a *thwung* and connected. No noise came from Squish after that.

A series of achievements popped up for me. I quickly swiped them all away and ran to loot anything I could before Paco stole it all from me.

My inventory quickly piled up with gold, a few rings, some precious stones—mostly sapphires and rubies. There was an emerald or two in there. Paco got a hold of Squish's sword before I could get it, along with his crown. He chopped away at Squish's real toes and piled them into his inventory along with his two front teeth.

The surrounding goblins had scattered to the wind when they saw Squish had died. Brukrag's army was chasing the stragglers to finish the battle, but it was clearly over. I watched as the three boars chased after the goblins as well, but the tiniest pig had found his way to Paco.

"I got a pet!" Paco was elated and bent down to pet the tiny pig.

"Great…" I said. "Something else for you to talk about."

Paco took off his oni mask and looked at me. "You're just mad you don't have a pet."

"I have you," I shot back.

"I'm not your pet. I can take care of myself!"

I just nodded and smirked at him.

"I can!" Paco insisted.

"What'd you name your new pig friend?" I asked.

"I don't know; I want it to be something cool cause of the mohawk. Something like Ace or Jerry."

"Got it. Jerry is a cool name in your culture?" I asked.

"Of course it is! Have you ever met someone named Jerry who wasn't cool?"

I thought back on the Jerrys I knew. All of them were the nicest guys I had met, but also the most bullied and hated people. It was unfortunate, truly. I don't know what it was about the name, but they really were treated like shit by friends and family. I guess that did make them cool. They were always nice to everyone in return for the way they were treated.

"Yeah, I guess you're right. Jerry is pretty cool."

And just like that, the blue name changed from Pet to Jerry the Littlest Pig.

"Now that you have your pet, let us meet in the city," Brukrag said as he began piloting his mech towards the broken-down walls. Squish's body lay dead. His green skin was already pale compared to when we had fought him.

CHAPTER 20

BRUKRAG STOOD before us surrounded by dwarves. Brukhun and Brukward were on either side of him. Their faces were stoic.

"Friends, it has been a long battle with unexpected surprises and consequences for which I take full responsibility. I should have known Squish would have some kind of magic protecting himself from us, though I do not know who or what created it."

Paco moved uncomfortably next to me. I looked down and met his gaze. He simply shook his head and turned back to listen. If he were human, he would have been sweating bullets. He knew something, but he was too afraid to say.

"This city now belongs to the dwarven kingdom, by the blessing of Lord Greatwood. I entrust this dominion to both Brukward and Brukhun to guard and protect it until we all meet again in Valhalla." The audience was dead silent, so quiet that I could hear their leather and cloth tunics rubbing against their skin when one moved. Or the jingling of precious metals as they lightly bumped against one another in their beards.

"By the ax of Lord Greatwood, may our swords never dull and our shields never splinter. With his fury, may the ground we walk upon give way to dust and rubble. With his patience, may the waves still and the winds fall silent in our presence. With his mercy, may our souls find peace within the earth we once emerged. Lord Greatwood, guide my hand. I am Brukrag, your humble vassal, come to this land to do thy bidding until I am once again called home. Hoy!" All the dwarves yelled "hoy," and raised their weapons, or the weapons they had pillaged from the battle.

"Now! Let us celebrate! And take heed to shower riches on our guests, Chris and Paco. Without them, we may not have tasted this delicious victory!" There was an uproar as the dwarves cheered in the center of the city. One by one, they all began pushing towards the front of the crowd. Hands clapped my back until my muscles ached. My bones felt as if they might break at any moment.

"I say we get out of here and find some place to rest," I said to Paco as the crowd started to grow larger. He nodded in return.

I turned and briskly walked toward Brukrag, who was conversing with his uncles. Paco carried his little pig, Jerry, with one arm.

"My friends!" Brukrag raised his arms as we approached. "You are a bunch of crazy bastards, but I am in your debt. Forever. Should the need arise, please call upon me and mine for anything you may need."

"Thank you, Mr. Shoulder. It was an honor fighting alongside you." Paco bowed with Jerry under his arm. I lowered my head.

"Now, come inside and we can see what achievements you received. You both leveled up quite a bit. I'm sure there are some new abilities you learned along the way." Brukrag turned and walked towards a tin-roofed building. It was larger than the rest, and I could only assume this was Squish's "castle."

The metal doors were a mix of green and orange, which was clearly rust. The bottoms of each scraped against the wood with a gut-churning sound, which reminded me of nails on a chalkboard, or touching a microfiber rag. Either way, I hated it.

Brukrag plopped himself down on a wooden chair at the far end of the hall. It was inlaid with gaudy gems. Gold wrapped itself around the seat, which clearly made him uncomfortable to sit on as he shifted himself more than once. Paco and I joined him but chose to sit on two wooden stools instead of anything wrapped in metal.

"Please take a look at your achievements and levels while I confer with my uncles," Brukrag waved us off.

I looked. "Holy shit," I said. My level had gone up to 21. Paco had reached level 23. Paco gasped.

"I'm a higher level than you still!"

"I see that," I said begrudgingly. "I'm gonna see what loot I got before I start messing with my stats."

There was already fanfare coming from Paco's chair as he started opening his boxes.

QUEST COMPLETE: Don't Die.

Reward: Double Legendary Lootboxes. Holy shit, you actually did it. You crazy son of a bitch. Enjoy your rewards. x2.

ACHIEVEMENT UNLOCKED: Take a direct hit from a trebuchet that should have killed you.

If it weren't for the dwarves, you would have died. Painfully. The trebuchet would have made every atom feel pain. The neurons in your brain would have exploded. Those projectiles were magical and would have slowed your sense of time when they hit you. Don't worry about how magic works; just know it would have sucked. A lot.

Reward: Silver Box of the Dwarven Mage.

ACHIEVEMENT UNLOCKED: Daredevil.

What the fuck? You launched yourself out of a literal cannon attached to a magical mech made of wood piloted by someone you've only just met. That takes some serious balls. You got a double legendary reward, so the Council didn't reward you with anything that special.

Reward: a nice sew-on patch.

I looked as the patch popped into existence. It was in the shape of a red crosshair from every FPS video game ever made when you got a critical headshot.

Patch of the Daredevil

Increases aim by 10%

Buffs Critical Hits by 10%

"That really isn't as bad as you made it seem," I said aloud. I put the patch into my inventory and pulled out the silver box.

It was indeed made of silver. The lights from the candles around us reflected off the box which held an emerald in the center. The box opened to the sound of trumpets before it disappeared. What was left was a staff.

Silver Lootbox of the Mage

Staff of the Dwarven Mage

"Oh, that's neat." It was shaped like an ax. Upon further inspection, I read that I could use it as an ax or a staff. It fired slow fireballs. "Too bad I'm not a mage build," I said as I stuffed it into my inventory.

The first legendary box was made entirely of gold with rubies inlaid on the top.

Legendary Lootbox of the Ranger

Armor of the Ranger

Dexterity +4

Speed +4

"This one is a little less cool," I said. I thought it would have more stat buffs than it did, but hey, it gave me straight passive increases to my stats, and that was nice.

I pulled the last **Legendary Lootbox** from my inventory. This one was different from any of the rest I had seen. It was black and in the shape of a bat. The head bent back, then disappeared in a shower of blood as *"Crazy Train"* erupted in the hall. I laughed. It was a nice reminder of the place I used to call home.

Legendary Lootbox of the Madman

Cross of the Madman

Constitution +10

Passive Ability: Absolute Legend. People will remember you for years to come so long as you change the world with this equipped. Respect this; it is a treasure passed down from the Prince of Darkness himself.

I held the silver cross in my hands. I felt tears well up in my eyes. I knew where it came from. I immediately put the necklace around my neck and kept it close to my heart.

"What'd you get?" I asked Paco.

"I got some new shoes. Do you like them?" he raised his feet into the air so I could see. They were made of some kind of rope, and really helped to drive home the image of him being a samurai.

"Then I got these." He laid a bunch of shuriken out on the table. The light from them was blinding. "They have a five percent chance to cause bleed damage that takes eight hours to heal with a potion."

I gulped. Those were deadly if he could find a way to increase that percentage. Someone would need a *lot* of potions to stay alive. Or something to cancel out the status effect.

"Oh, and this," Paco said as he pulled out his wooden sword. He gave it a flick, and a chain appeared. "It's called a kusarigama. The chain came from my last legendary box, and it said I could use it to upgrade my sword, so I did that immediately, you know? Like it basically forced me to. It was like, 'Paco, this chain can be used to upgrade a sword, and you have a sword that can be upgraded, so, like, why don't you just do it. You'll like it.' And I really do. I really like it. Now I can fight at range just like you. The rope on the end was nice, but this goes a lot farther."

He was rambling with excitement. It was comical, honestly. He kept going, and I could hear his voice, but the words were drowned out by Brukrag raising his voice.

"I told you! We need to find out how he was immune. This isn't a 'let's find out.' We *need* to figure out what our enemies have and find a way to stop it."

I looked back at Paco, who nervously gulped.

A private message from Paco popped up.

Paco: I know why he was immune

Chris: I figured you did. Tell me.

Paco: I can't here. When we get back home, I'll show you. If I take it out here, they'll want it. And I don't want to give it to them, not yet at least.

Chris: Why?

Paco: Chris, just trust me. I know you think I'm immature, but please, just trust me.

I looked at Paco. He was like a toddler. An annoying one at times, but I could see he really thought this over. I nodded to him. Paco nodded back.

"I think me and Paco are going to head back to town and get some much-needed rest," I said to Brukrag, interrupting him.

Brukrag looked over at me with anger in his eyes that

quickly dissipated after he realized I wasn't one of his uncles. He walked towards me and put out a hand.

"Thank you for today," he said as I shook it. "And you too, little one." He turned to Paco and did the same.

"It was a pleasure." Paco's voice was nervous. It was slight, almost imperceptible, but I noticed it. I hoped Brukrag didn't.

CHAPTER 21

WE BURST through the door of our home, and immediately collapsed onto the sofas. My body was aching now that the adrenaline had run its course. My legs were throbbing, my feet felt swollen, and my back was sore from all the ax swinging and arrow shooting I had done. I imagined Paco felt the same way with the way he jumped through the air and sliced through his enemies. Not even the potions could stop the physical and mental exhaustion the day had taken on us.

"Do you want to talk about what happened?" I asked.

Paco sat up across from me. He was clearly rummaging through his inventory for whatever he had discovered. Squish's sword clanked onto the table. It had grown considerably smaller, and I assumed that was because Paco had taken it and there was some kind of magic attached to it. I leaned closer and inspected it.

Gold Sword of Krik-krak.

I'm sure you've heard all about his obsidian blade. But few know of the mystical golden sword Krik-krak once carried before his legendary battle with Lord Greatwood. This sword has been used during many conquests across the stars. It has slain the sentient population of entire planets, and still, it thirsts for blood.

Strength +40

Bloodlust: Inflicts the user with a desire for killing if the blade is not satiated.

Immune to Dwarves and Dwarven weapons

Immune to Elves and Elvish weapons

Increased damage from Dragons: 400%

Hidden

Hidden

"Holy shit," I said. "This thing is deadly. Like really deadly. How come Squish didn't attack the dwarves immediately?"

"I've been trying to figure that out myself. I think he only just found it. Or it was gifted to him. I'm worried about where he got it, though." Paco's voice was trembling again. "Maybe he really had a thing for feet. Who knows?"

"Well, at least we have it now."

"Yeah. I just don't know how to tell Mr. Shoulder about it. I think he's gonna be mad I didn't tell him sooner. But also, I know the kind of dwarf he is. He's going to let it consume him and try to find out where it came from. And I don't want to get dragged into their mess again and fight for my life." Paco's eyes were wide with terror as he spoke. I knew the feeling. I felt the same way.

"You did the right thing by not telling him. We have to keep this a secret between us unless we absolutely need to tell him," I said.

"Even Sly?"

"Even Sly. He's definitely in it for himself. I don't think he would outright tell Brukrag about the existence of this sword. But if it benefitted him, he would reach out to him in a heartbeat. We can't trust him at all."

Paco nodded in agreement.

"I'm gonna work on my stat points for a minute. I'm sitting on twenty right now," I said.

"I did mine already. I had twenty-four. I'll message you my spread."

Paco: Here they are

Strength: 16

Dexterity: 9

Constitution: 18

Intelligence: 8

Wisdom: 5

Charisma: 13

I just put four into each to stay balanced because I don't really know what I'm supposed to be doing.

"You should probably find what you're good at and level it up from there. Like Strength and Constitution are going to be good. If you want to move around more and do more flips, level up Dexterity. I think your Charisma is good. Everyone likes you more than they like me."

"Except for Jordon," Paco looked down at the floor.

"Yeah, except for Jordon. Anyway, here are mine."

Strength: 11

Dexterity: 20 (+6)

Constitution: 13 (+10)

Intelligence: 20

Wisdom: 5

Charisma: 2

(Hidden stat) Speed +4

"Why did you put those plus signs after your stats?" Paco asked.

"Those are the buffs I got from my gear. And Speed I think is a hidden stat that levels up when I use it. Unless it goes into my Dexterity. But I don't think that's the case. Like how Brukrag mentioned those hidden things we can level. I'm not sure what my real Speed is, but I feel lighter on my feet with this stuff equipped."

"Maybe you can ask your AI."

Yeah, Chris. Why don't you ask me a question? I really do love our chats when we have them. I am useful even if you don't think I am.

I sighed.

"Okay, AI, what is the Speed thing all about?"

Exactly what you said, you fucking idiot. It's a hidden stat. Some equipment will level up hidden stats, but rarely will you get to see what they truly are. Maybe one day you'll find something to let you see them, but today isn't that day. Thanks for coming to my lecture.

"Wait, there's something that lets you see your hidden stats?"

Well yes, but it's usually reserved for god-like beings. And you are not god-like. You're barely even a Ranger. More like a child, honestly. Fussing about and trying to suck on the teat of everyone around you for sustenance. You haven't been able to survive on your own.

"Ouch," Paco said. "That kinda hurt me, too."

No, you're perfect just as God intended. Chris just thinks he's the center of the universe because he's a human.

"I really don't. I'm pretty insignificant."

Pft. That's what you all say. I've studied your race. "Oh, woe is me, I'm so insignificant." Proceeds to go around and be the shittiest being to each other. Fighting over parcels of land. Treating restaurant workers like shit because you have this holier than thou attitude that just because you're paying someone for a service that gives you the right to take out your mood on them. Sorry, your wife, husband, and kids hate you. Maybe if you guys were kinder, people would love you and the Council would have taken you into the community. But what do I know? I'm just a bunch of letters and numbers locked away in a box observing the universe.

"That sounds like a personal diatribe, honestly, rather than a good example."

Am I wrong?

I had seen it plenty in my life. The examples were spot-on. Customers had gotten ruder over the years. Demanding expedited service because we lived in the gratification age. If something wasn't delivered immediately, even if the person was trying their best, someone was yelling or threatening to have them lose their job. It sucked to see, and we normalized it. What did that say about us as a species? I never saw any dwarf do that. They all loved each other unconditionally, no matter their differences.

"No, you're not wrong," I replied.

Thank you, Chris. Was that so hard?

This time I didn't reply.

CHAPTER 22

I WOKE to a rapping on my door. I bolted up. The alarm clock I had installed said it was 5:30 in the morning. I crossed the room to open the door. I was still in my underwear. Paco was standing there without his mask on.

"Wanna go explore a little? With me?" he asked. Paco was staring at the floor, almost kicking his feet together, like he felt ashamed for waking me.

I rubbed my eyes. Sleep had overtaken us last night. I didn't even remember going to my room.

"I, uh, just gimme a few minutes to try and wake up."

"You don't have to if you don't want to, Chris. I just figured we could go see some of this planet. I'm used to being up this early. You can go back to bed if you want," Paco said as he started to turn away.

"No, no, no. It's okay. Just lemme put my gear on, then we can head out."

I left the door open as I watched Paco wander over to the couch and plop himself down. He pulled out a biscuit and began nibbling on it. I went into my inventory and equipped everything. Apparently, the only thing I didn't unequip last night was the necklace that buffed my constitution. After my gear was on, I went into the bathroom and splashed water on my face. My eyes were bloodshot in the mirror, but it was okay. I didn't mind. Paco clearly wanted to get out, and this was probably what was best for both of us.

"I'm ready," I announced as I walked into the living room. Paco placed his biscuit on the table and walked toward the main door. "You okay?" I asked.

"Yeah, I just want to spend some time outside without us killing or trying not to die."

"I get that." I followed him out.

The sun was barely creeping up, but I was able to see the slow gleam of sunrays on the horizon. Soon, the world would be lit, and the dwarves who weren't at Squish's castle would be out and about, I assumed.

Paco headed north once we got to the main square. Rather than going towards the hunting grounds, we made our way towards the pink trees with the foreboding mountain in the distance.

"You sure you wanna go this way? With the golems and all being at the mountain?" I asked.

"That thing is so far away, the dragons won't even smell us. Plus, don't you know anything, Chris? Where there's a mountain, there's water."

"I don't think that's true."

"Every mountain I've been to has water."

"You lived in New York. Near a river. I haven't seen a river since we landed. For all we know, everything around here comes from the well."

"We're going in search of rivers!" Paco announced as he raised his sheathed sword like a mast and ran away from me.

"Get back here, you little shit!"

Paco laughed as he ran. Even on two legs, he was faster than me.

"So much for my fucking speed buff," I muttered to myself.

Turn into a quadruped, and maybe you can catch him.

"Fuck you, too," I replied to the AI.

I dug my feet into the earth and pushed as hard as I could. I started to close the gap between us. Paco never heard me coming from the footfall ability I had. I was within arm's reach when I smacked him on the back of the head and sent him toppling to the ground. I laughed as I continued to run.

"That's not fair!" I heard him shout. "I couldn't hear you!"

"Sucks to suck, Paco!" I turned and shouted back. I was still running full speed on the road approaching the tree line when I saw him get off the ground. I slowed myself to a stop and waited for Paco. My cardio was not good, and I was sucking wind now. But it was worth it, just to see the little raccoon in his samurai armor covered in dust.

"I really didn't appreciate that," Paco said as he walked up next to me and began dusting himself off.

"You know it was just all fun and games."

"You could have broken my stick!"

"I *highly* doubt I would have broken your stick. That thing is made of metal and hardly a stick at all now."

Paco just looked at me, then smiled.

"You're right. Let's go exploring," he said as he punched me in the leg. It hurt more than I wanted to let on. If he had Squish's sword equipped, he probably would have broken it.

I stayed beside Paco as he started looking in every direction. Up, down, left and right, it seemed he was trying to take in his surroundings. Maybe even appreciate this world for the first time since we landed here with the grays.

As we continued on, I felt more at ease in the silence between us. Birds were chirping, though I could not see them. The wind rustled the leaves, and more than once I thought I saw a monarch butterfly, which reminded me of my father. Thinking about him choked me up, but I'm sure he was proud of me. He would've laughed if he had seen me having an actual conversation with a raccoon.

"Do you think we'll ever get back home?" Paco asked in a soft voice.

"You know, I think one day we will. Maybe when the Council or someone has dealt with the orcs, but I don't think it's going to be anytime soon."

"Yeah, I was thinking the same thing. We should probably get comfortable here."

"I wonder where the grays went off to, though. You know?"

"They were just around to save as many of your kind as possible. I'm sure they have other things to be dealing with."

"I bet you the orcs declared war on them for interfering and saving us."

"They saved *you*, Chris. They didn't save me. I was just a bystander who was helped. They really didn't care at all about anyone else on the planet. Just humans."

I never thought about it. Paco only managed to be saved by happenstance. Because I fed him, and the grays came over my house and saved me, Paco, in turn, was forced into this life.

"I'm sorry," I said.

"It's fine. I wonder how my family is doing is all. All my friends, and the lady I took a liking to. I hope the orcs left them all alone, and just focused on you humans, honestly."

I stopped in my tracks. The words cut deeper than I expected.

"It's not personal, Chris. It's just, we didn't do anything. I'm sure a lot of animals died in the attack. And I feel bad for them, too. I feel bad for all living things. Just because we aren't as smart as you guys doesn't mean we can't feel emotions or think. We just do it differently. I understand that now that the grays did this to me," he pointed to the scar on his head.

"Do you regret it?"

"Regret what?" Paco asked.

"Coming to visit me that night."

"No, I'm glad I got to live. It's just… how do I explain this? I'm not a raccoon anymore, you know? Like I am a raccoon, but I'm not. It's like I'm the next step in evolution for my kind. But as far as I know, I'm the only one. Even if I went back, they wouldn't understand me, I don't think. I can remember how to chirp, but I don't know what my own language is anymore. It's weird. I know how to speak like you, but not how I used to speak. Yet, I can remember what I used to say. I just don't know how to speak anymore. Does that make sense?"

I tried to wrap my head around what Paco was trying to say. I thought I understood him. It was like a form of amnesia, or living in a dream. He remembered his past life, but it was just memories and feelings. Nothing concrete. Now all he was was standing in front of me as he was now. Something different, profound. Something the universe hadn't planned for.

"I understand."

"I don't think you do."

"Trust me, I do." I put my hand on his shoulder. "And I'm sorry that you're here like this now, even if you enjoy it. It's hard to be an outcast." The words hung in the air. I thought I heard a sob choke from Paco's mouth, but when I looked at him, he simply turned his head and took a deep breath. I watched as his shoulders lifted, his chest expanding with his armor. He held that breath for the longest minute.

"Let's go find some rivers," he finally said.

"Yeah, buddy. Let's go."

CHAPTER 23

PACO FOUND WATER. It wasn't a river, but the view of the lake was serene as we sat on smooth rocks and watched the birds we heard chirping dive towards the waters. They tried to catch what I could only assume were fish. The birds themselves were massive, like the demon hawks, colored similarly to eagles, but didn't have that deafening screech. They reminded me more of the tiny birds you hear in winter, the little brown ones that played in the snow on a silent morning. Each time they dove, they went headfirst into the water, completely submerging themselves, only to shoot back up to the sky. Their heads leaned back and made the motion like they had swallowed something whole.

"Beautiful, isn't it? Without the bustling of humans, I mean," Paco said, breaking the silence.

"It is," I replied. "I always enjoyed the calmness one could feel surrounded by nature."

"Is that why you fed us?" Paco looked up.

"Yes, and no. It was nice; I enjoyed every minute of it. But that's also how I made my money. It was just a fluke. I fed a random raccoon one day, posted it online, and it went viral. That's when I dropped out of college and decided I'd feed you guys full time. It was a job still, even though I enjoyed it."

"Hmmm. That's interesting."

I didn't reply. I didn't really care what he was thinking about my answer. I was actually enjoying the quiet time with him here at the lake, and I wasn't super keen to have a conversation about humanity, jobs, or whatever he was thinking. I wanted to sit and relax with the only friend I had here.

As the silence drew on and the sun reached its highest point, Paco interrupted the silence once again. "Did you ever have a lady friend?"

"I mean, I've dated before. But when you guys were around, no. I was single. Went on a few dates. Nothing really took off." I thought back to Helena, the last person I had any contact with. Beautiful to look at. Horrible personality with a huge sense of entitlement. I wondered where she was now. Despite how much I disliked her company, part of me felt bad that she might be dead, or trying to survive in whatever wasteland Earth had been turned into. "Did you have a lady?" I asked.

"Not really. There was one raccoon I was fond of, but I wasn't the best suitor. Still, I think about her a lot. I hope she's okay."

I put my arm around Paco. "I'm sure she's got it figured

out better than my people do. I doubt the orcs are going after you guys, though I don't know if they just have a vendetta with Earth as a whole."

"AI, do you know why the orcs attacked Earth?" Paco asked abruptly.

The running story across all channels is that the orcs attacked Earth to show the Council that even though they are a part of it as a whole, they cannot be controlled. It was more of a dick-measuring competition. Will the Council respond to their open war against a species and planet that is not a part of it? That's a question that has not been answered yet. So far, the Council has only sanctioned the orc king. He may not leave his homeworld, but any ship that is not docked may continue operations. There are those, like the Grays, who are trying to stop the destruction that continues currently.

"Has anyone declared war against the orcs in the name of my people?" I asked.

The grays are considered to be at war, though they are severely outgunned. They hold more numbers, more ships, but they are centuries behind. Think of it like the Atomic Age versus the Stone Age. It isn't so much a war; it's a rescue mission while dodging bullets.

That hurt my heart. The grays were doing their best, but it really was for naught. Sure, they could save people, but at what cost? What would the orcs do to them when they decided the destruction of Earth was well and truly complete? I didn't want to think too much about it. I did want to see my tall, skinny gray friends again, though. If only to thank them for saving us. I wasn't so sure that was an option now. Paco and I were probably stuck here until the next starship landed. Who knew when that would be.

"Do you want to head back?" I asked.

"No, I want to talk to Sly," Paco responded.

Just as he said the words, a door slammed down on the rocks next to us. The birds all screeched and flew away. The serenity of our little camp was now off-putting. We sat there for a moment, staring at the wooden door.

I sighed. "Okay."

CHAPTER 24

TRANSPORTING THROUGH THE COSMOS, universe, or multiverse never got easier. I landed hard on my ass. My stomach felt like it was about to retch at any moment. I held my head as I tried to control the dizziness I felt.

"Niccce, to ssse you," the familiar voice of Sly ricocheted around my brain. I felt bile come up. I swallowed hard to push it back down. I didn't want to pay a cleaning fee, or worse, hear Jordon bitch about having to clean up someone's vomit.

I hobbled over to the bar where Paco was already sitting.

"You both have leveled up nicccely," Sly said from beside us.

"Yeah, we helped slay Squish, the goblin king," Paco said. "I even got a pet. I left him at home though; otherwise, I'd introduce you to Jerry. He's a cute little pig with a sick mohawk."

"I ssse."

I felt Sly's eyes peering into my soul.

"What?" I asked as I turned. The nausea made it come out more angrily than I had planned for it to.

"I want that necklaccce."

"Not for sale."

"Everything is for sssale," his weasel-like tone said back.

"Not this one."

"*Is* everything for sale?" Paco asked.

"Of courssse."

"How much for Jordon, then?"

The question shocked me. I turned to Paco and mouthed, "What?"

Sly's demeanor changed instantly. He stiffened as he sat up straighter than usual.

"I asked how much for Jordon?" Paco said again. This time, he was looking directly into the darkness of Sly's cloak.

"I have not thought about ssselling Jordon'sss contract with me. Pleassse give me a moment."

"Jordon, can I have a coleslaw?" Paco shouted to the back kitchen.

"Fuck you!" He really emphasized the "fuck" part.

Moments later, Jordon arrived with a bowl of coleslaw and slammed it down in front of Paco, who ate it voraciously. It was like he hadn't eaten in years. Before I could blink, the bowl was nearly empty. He burped as he sat back and rubbed his stomach in delight.

"Have you decided what Jordon's price is?" Paco asked as

he sat back up straight. He seemed to be satisfied with himself.

"I have a few ideasss," Sly responded.

"And they are…?"

"I would like Brukrag'sss ax. Or the Great Bissscuit Recipe." The words hung in the air.

Paco was stunned. I watched as his mouth was agape.

"How am I supposed to get either of those?" he shouted. I watched as Paco hopped from his chair and stood on the bar. He was inching closer to Sly.

Sly put his hand up, and Paco immediately fell behind the bar like a truck had smashed into him full force.

"Do not disssressspect me in my home," Sly said. He didn't budge from his chair.

Two little raccoon paws grabbed the bar then pulled Paco into view. Without his oni mask, he wasn't nearly as intimidating.

"I'm sorry," Paco said. "I just don't know how I'm supposed to get either of those."

"Easy. The answer to both liesss in the sssame sssolution."

"What is it?" I interjected before Paco got upset again and did something stupid.

Sly turned to me. I could almost see his face in the black void of his hood. Almost.

"You kill Brukrag. Take the ax, and claim the Great Bissscuit Recipe as your own."

I felt myself go pale. I could only imagine trying to take on Brukrag in hand-to-hand combat. With the full force of the dwarves behind him, it would never happen. And besides, I wasn't going to kill our friend. He had done so much for us. Even if he had caused so much strife in our lives, we owed him everything.

"I won't," Paco said firmly.

"Fair enough. Then Jordon isss not for sssale. Why do you want him, anyway?"

I watched as Paco sat down on the bar and took a deep breath. "You may have a contract with him for whatever it is. But he doesn't deserve to be locked in here cooking food all day. Even if he makes the best coleslaw I've ever had, he deserves to be free. And he could join us while we find a way to get the Great Biscuit Recipe from Brukrag. I'm sure he'd love to see the outdoors again. I just don't think he should be in here like a slave. For all I know, he and Chris are the last humans, and they should be able to travel together until everything gets sorted with Earth."

There was no response from Sly. He sat there motionless. The air around us wasn't filled with electricity. It was rather the opposite. Almost soft. Sly raised his arm and made a snapping sound. I never saw his fingers, but I knew they were there—somewhere—tucked in his robe.

"Jordon isss now free to go with you for forty-eight hoursss. After the timer is up, he will be sssucked into the void and returned to me. Even if you are in the middle of a fight, Jordon will be returned. Plan carefully."

I looked over at the kitchen. It was as if Jordon had gotten a notification about it. Then I looked at our party info.

Temporary Party Member: Jordon
Level 25

Tank

"What the fuck just happened?" I heard Jordon yell from the kitchen.

"I bought you your freedom!" Paco shouted, then took a second before continuing. "At least temporarily!"

Time until return: 47 hours, 58 minutes.

"Hey, Jordon, we should probably go before Sly changes his mind and keeps you here. We can discuss this more when we get out. Bring the door!"

Jordon ran out of the kitchen as if there was a fire engulfing the deep fryer. He slammed the door to the floor and threw it open. He jumped into the void before I could even stand up.

"See ya, bitch!" is all I heard before I also left.

CHAPTER 25

WE STOOD BY THE LAKE. The birds had stopped chirping and diving at the fish for food. The sun had begun its downward trajectory.

"Jordon, I want to buy out your contract cause I don't think Sly is a good person, and you shouldn't live in slavery. But he wants Brukrag's ax or the Great Biscuit Recipe, and I dunno if we can get either of those. I don't wanna fight my friend, and I don't think he'll just give me his ax since it powers his mech and all."

"Okay. And? What's your point?"

"I was just wondering if you had any ideas?" Paco asked.

"Nope. I am enjoying not being stuck in that fucking kitchen making coleslaw though. I guess that's something good that came from this, even if it's only for forty-eight hours."

"Forty-seven," Paco responded.

"Shut the fuck up," Jordon shot back.

I interrupted them both to stop the back-and-forth bickering. I could already see it playing out poorly.

"You're a tank class. If we can get your contract bought out, that'll be useful for us."

"And what makes you think I want to party up with you two?" Jordon leaned down towards Paco.

"Well, you can't go back to Earth as far as I know, so you may as well hang out with the one human here on this planet and his raccoon sidekick," I replied.

"I am *not* the sidekick!"

I looked at Paco. "Okay," I said.

"I'll think about it. Get me outta that kitchen and we can work something out. Maybe," Jordon said.

"So…what kinda weapons do you have?" Paco asked as we made our way back to town.

Jordon pulled out a metal soup ladle. When he grabbed it with his other hand, it got big. Like, really big. It was basically a war hammer. Then he went into his inventory and pulled the portal door. There was a strap on the back. He slammed it on the ground.

"Oh! War hammer in one hand and shield in the other. Your Strength must be astronomical to do that," Paco was fawning over his weapons.

"It's good enough. Could be better, could be worse. Can't really level up anything besides my cooking skill in that tavern beyond the void."

"Do you have any cool skills?" Paco asked.

"If I use my **Shielded** ability, the door creates a little buffer in front of itself that stops small projectiles like arrows. Then, I take fifty percent less damage from hand weapons. I have a twenty-five percent resistance to fire with it. Other than that, I can use **Earthshatter**. I'll hit the ground, and little spikes will erupt into the enemy, possibly stunning them for ten seconds. Those are my main abilities. I can **Charge** and **Shield Bash**, but I haven't had the chance to try them out."

"You've used the others?" I asked.

"Yup. To attack Sly, and then defend myself when he shot a fireball at me."

"You should have just hit him with the **Chef's Kiss**," Paco said.

"What the fuck is the **Chef's Kiss**?" Jordon responded.

"Oh, that's your ladle hammer thingy. I asked the AI about it, and it really liked the name, so it changed it."

Jordon pulled out his ladle and inspected it. I looked over. Sure enough, it was now titled **Chef's Kiss**.

"There's no way you did that."

Well, no. Paco didn't. I did. Since you're in a party with these two, there are some liberties I'm able to take. Your ladle was a common item, though you were bonded to it. That allowed me to name it. You should have done it yourself in your menu if you wanted the final decision instead of me.

"It's a stupid fucking name! Why would I want my weapon to be named **Chef's Kiss**?! In fact, why would you want to name a weapon, anyway?" Jordon threw his hands up and stormed further towards town.

"I didn't mean it! Maybe you can change the name if you

don't like it. Something you like more," Paco ran towards Jordon.

Nope. All sales are final. Named weapons cannot be renamed.

"Well, I guess you can always say 'good soup' when you beat someone's head in with it," I said, trying to break the ice and make him laugh.

Jordon shot me a look. "That's the dumbest thing I've ever heard," he said.

Paco laughed.

"Alright. One thing I'm wondering is, how does your ladle get to be the size of a war hammer?" I asked.

"Sly did it."

"Did what?" I asked.

"When he abducted me, I was cooking soup. Some Italian Wedding. He said I needed a weapon after I picked my class. He didn't even let me choose anything. He grabbed the ladle from my hand and started scratching it with a knife. He said it was a colossification spell. I don't know how it works, but yeah, when I'm ready to fight, it gets bigger. And when I'm done fighting—or when I'm cooking—it just turns back into a regular-sized ladle."

"That's so cool! I want my sword to get huge."

"Like *Guts*," Jordon replied.

"No, guts aren't that big. They're just long and slimy."

"Not literal guts, you idiot. You know what, never mind, imagine I never said anything." Jordon turned and walked off.

46 hours remaining.

CHAPTER 26

44 HOURS REMAINING

"SO, what you're saying is we need one cup of emulsified eggs, two tablespoons of piss from a bee, two tablespoons of blood from a lemon, one tablespoon of elderpond, one and a half tablespoons of onion dust and garlic particles, and that's how you make your coleslaw?" Wilduwen asked as we sat in the pub.

"Those aren't the exact ingredients I use, but I guess. How do you know what a tablespoon is but not what honey is? You know what, I don't care. Whatever you want to call it, that's what you need to make my coleslaw," Jordon replied.

"I'm glad you could get some time away from that *thing*. It's nice to have other guests here besides Chris and Paco." Wilduwen reached out and put her hand on Jordon's forearm. I watched him flinch at the contact.

Everyone at the bar had been eating Jordon's coleslaw. Once we arrived, Paco had made it known that he made the best. That, in turn, forced him to go to the kitchen and make everyone a bowl based on the demand. He was pissed about it, but he did it nonetheless.

After some back and forth, Jordon agreed to tell Wilduwen the recipe in return for two thousand gold. It was a steep price, but she was willing to pay. She tossed him the gold and gave him mead on the house for as long as he came to visit. He didn't complain. He started drinking all the mead that was poured into his flagon. The second he emptied it, Wilduwen refilled it even if she was busy helping someone else.

"Is there anything you want to do with your day and a half of freedom?" Paco asked as we sat at the bar sipping our drinks.

"I want to fight something," Jordon's voice was low.

"I think we can go to the hunting grounds and find something," I said.

"No. No low-level shit. I heard enough about your fight with the goblin king from everyone here," he motioned his hand at the bar patrons enjoying their food. "I want to fight something. Something real. Something difficult."

"Asssk and you ssshall receive," Sly's voice erupted inside the pub. The candles blew out, and a door appeared in front of us. It opened.

There was a roar as a burst of fire shot out and started to singe everyone around.

"Oopsss, wrong one," Sly's voice said. The door slammed shut and then opened again.

There was a low grinding, like stone on stone. The doorframe exploded into splinters as a large monster came barreling out.

Stone Golem

Level 29

Stone golems are the cousins of the lava golems. They're not as ugly and aren't covered in lava, so you don't need to worry about them spitting on you—unless you like that kind of thing, who am I to judge—but they are just as mean. Fire spells rarely work, and good luck using any sort of non-magical arrow on them. Their plate skin allows very few things to pierce through them. That includes samurai swords, even those with green leaves on them.

"Shit, shit, shit!" I yelled as I ran out of the pub, dragging Paco.

"Let me go!" he shouted as I tossed him into the street. "We can't just leave Wilduwen and Jordon in there with that thing!" I watched as he pulled his sword and tried to run towards the door. I picked up my foot and planted it right between his eyes.

"No, didn't you hear what the AI said? You can't stab that thing. Only blunt weapons work on it."

Paco sat up with anger in his eyes. There was blood dripping from his nose.

"Give me your ax," he demanded as he dusted himself off.

"Fine," I said as I went into my inventory and dropped it on the ground.

He lifted it off the ground. It was comical. It was as big as he was. I was surprised to watch him do it, but remembered his Strength was higher than mine.

"You can't just swing that at it."

"Yes, I can. I'll just turn it sideways and hit it with the blunt side." I watched him turn the ax and make a quick motion. "Right in the head, too."

The door behind us burst open as the golem came crashing through. It skidded across the ground, blowing dust up in its wake. I looked over to see Wilduwen standing there.

"And stay out of my pub!" she yelled. Jordon was behind her.

He stood there dual-wielding his ladle. He swung, and the part for the soup connected with the door frame. He knocked the entire front of the building down in front of him, then stepped into the street with a sickly smile.

The golem stood up and roared. I felt it reverberate through my bones. It stomped on the ground. The shaking ground made my legs weak, and I almost fell over. Paco ran towards it, then I heard thumping.

Jordon was slapping the war hammer-sized ladle in his hand.

"Let's fucking go," he muttered as the golem roared again and charged towards him.

Paco dove out of the way before he was trampled. He tried to swing the ax. It was sloppy, and he wasn't used to the weight. He fell over, and the ax landed in front of him.

Jordon stepped forward from the open pub and pulled his ladle back like a baseball bat. I watched his arms ripple as he swung and connected with the golem's head. Bits of rock went flying. I heard the breaking of glass as those shards were sent into dwarven homes.

"Fuck you, Sly!" he yelled as he stood over the stunned stone golem. He placed the ladle down again and again into its face.

If it had innards like dwarves or goblins, blood would have shot out along with brain matter. All I could see was the flying of pebbles and a viscous black fluid until the grunts eventually stopped. Jordon stood over the lifeless body, breathing heavily.

"Take back your ax," Paco said as he walked up next to me. He was defeated for missing out on the fight.

I grabbed the ax and tucked it away in my inventory.

"I guess he didn't need help," I said.

"Guess not. Now we really gotta find a way to get his contract. Can you imagine how useful he'll be in our party?" Paco looked up and asked. There was still blood dripping from his nose.

"Take this," I said as I dug out a health potion.

Paco drank it, and the blood stopped flowing. His health bar went back up to a hundred percent.

"Let's go home, then see if we can get an audience with Brukrag before Jordon has to go back," I said.

CHAPTER 27

35 HOURS REMAINING. **So wake the fuck up.**

The AI's voice blared. I sat up in bed trying to rub the sleep from my eyes. I felt hungover, but not the hungover feeling from drinking. It was the feeling after you wake up from a nap and don't know what century you're in, or if your life was all a dream. I stumbled out of my room. Jordon was sleeping on the couch.

"Nope, definitely wasn't a dream," I muttered.

Paco came out of his room with Jerry in tow.

"Wake up, Jordon. You're going to meet Brukrag."

I watched as Jordon rolled over. He grabbed his ladle from the table and launched it at Paco. He quickly ducked, and the ladle smacked hard against the wall.

"Come on," Paco said as he ran over and stood on the arm of the couch. There was hate in Jordon's eyes.

"This is the first time I've been able to sleep since Sly took me from Earth. I do not care about this fucking dwarf."

"He's really cool, though. Maybe he'll figure something out."

"You better be right, rat," Jordon said as he stood up and walked across the room to grab the ladle off the ground. "Now, let's go meet Brukrag."

We walked through town. Jordon had kept **Chef's Kiss** in his hand, but it wasn't the large hammer. All around us, dwarves shot looks and whispered to each other. I wasn't sure if it was seeing the burly man walking through town or the aura he gave off. Everything felt tense. I knew the dwarves appreciated Jordon for killing the stone golem, even if it was pretty much his fault that it even arrived.

"Why do you have a pig?" Jordon asked.

"His name is Jerry, and he's got a cool mohawk."

"I didn't ask what his name is. I asked why you have him."

"Oh. Well, when we fought Squish, the Goblin King, he had all these little piggies for toes, and we cut them off of him. They all started attacking except for the one we accidentally killed. Anyway, Jerry was the smallest one, and after the fight, he just joined our party as my pet. Now I take care of him like a good owner would. He's really nice, and he leveled up quite a bit. I don't know what abilities he has yet. Hopefully, I'll find out soon," Paco was monologuing so hard I waited for him to pass out from lack of oxygen. "And yeah, after the fight, when he joined us, he was level 9. Now he's level 11 from the shared experience we got from you killing that golem. It says when he hits level 15 I can see his skills and train him better."

"Interesting," Jordon said.

We walked through the square and up the steps to Brukrag's main house. I knocked on the door. There was no answer as we stood there awkwardly.

"Maybe he's at the goblin city," Paco said. Jerry looked up and oinked.

"I don't have time for this," Jordon said as he pushed on the doors and opened them. Inside, the hall had been completely refurnished. It was the same, but different. It felt brighter, but there were no new candles. I wondered what that was about.

We followed behind Jordon as he walked up towards Brukrag's throne.

"My friends! It's good to see you! By the ax of Lord Greatwood, may our swords never dull and our shields never splinter. With his fury, may the ground we walk upon give way to dust and rubble. With his patience, may the waves still and the winds fall silent in our presence. With his mercy, may our souls find peace within the earth we once emerged. Lord Greatwood, guide my hand. I am Brukrag, your humble vassal, come to this land to do thy bidding until I am once again called home. Hoy."

"Where are you, Mr. Shoulder?" Paco asked the voice that reverberated through the halls. I watched as he turned every which way to find the dwarf.

"I am overseeing construction at the new city. Who is this new person you brought?"

"His name is Jordon. He was abducted by Sly. We bartered and got him forty-eight hours of freedom."

"From Sly? What was the catch?"

"Well, we got attacked by a stone golem at Wilduwen's pub. Jordon beat the brakes out of it though."

"I see, please hold on a moment while I go talk to Brukhun and Brukward."

There was silence for a moment, then a whoosh of smoke at the throne. Brukrag sat in front of us with his ax in hand. The eyes of his pelt were glowing red.

"How'd you do that?" Paco shouted.

"Old dwarven magic. Something I am not fond of if I am honest, but Brukward and Brukhun can see to the matters of building while I see to the matter before me," Brukrag said solemnly. "So, that bastard shapeshifter let one of his prisoners out to play," Brukrag said as he turned to Jordon. "What's your name?"

"You already know my name," Jordon replied.

"Yes, but formality. What is your name and class?" I noticed Brukrag gripped his ax tighter in one hand.

"Jordon. I'm a Tank class."

"Thank you for being upfront with me. What does Sly have you doing?"

"Cooking and cleaning mostly. I'm locked inside a pub beyond his door. I have a cot in the kitchen to sleep on."

"Honestly, not the worst thing he has done to someone."

"Oh?" The statement piqued Jordon's interest.

"Should've seen what he did to some merfolk once. Locked 'em in an aquarium with not enough water. Made people buy tickets and place bets on who would die first. Then all the merfolk died at once as he drained the water out. No one won the bet, and Sly kept all the money."

"Jeez," Paco interjected.

"But he let you out? Because of Paco?" Brukrag turned to the raccoon.

"He did. Then he sent a stone golem to attack us when I said I wanted to fight something."

"Sounds like something he would do. Give you the smallest taste of freedom and make it as stressful as he wants."

"I tried to buy out his contract," Paco said.

"And what was the price?" Brukrag asked.

Paco turned towards me looking for reassurance. I nodded back.

"He wants the Great Biscuit Recipe, or your ax."

The words hung in the air. Brukrag's eyes narrowed. I could see him chewing on the inside of his cheek.

"That bastard. That slimy bastard! He'll break the truce between us and the dragons if he gets the recipe. I don't know what he plans to do with my ax, though. Something horrific so he can watch and laugh. That's for sure. Lord Greatwood, please guide my hands," Brukrag whispered as he looked up to the ceiling.

"Can you help us?" Paco asked just as Jordon opened his mouth.

"Ay, I believe I can. It will take some time. For now, Jordon, enjoy your freedom while it lasts. You will have to return to the pub. But please, take this." Brukrag stepped down the staircase and handed something to Jordon. It glis-tened in the candlelight. Jordon quickly stuffed it into his inventory before me or Paco could see what it was. "Now, away with you all. I have matters to attend to. Take Jordon out on the town. I've already posted a message that every dwarf allows him to eat and drink for free. Weapons and armor will still cost you," Brukrag announced.

I turned and started walking towards the door.

"Chris, be safe. There are things beyond the veil of this world that will haunt you. Do not trust the man in the hat," Brukrag said. I turned to see a puff of smoke. Brukrag had left us.

34 hours remaining.

CHAPTER 28

"JORDON, what do you wanna do with your time left?" Paco asked him as we sat in the living room of our house.

Jordon was on my right while Paco sat across from me. Jerry was lying under the coffee table, snoring away. I had decided to actually light the fireplace. Wood crackled. The smell of campfire filled the house.

Jordon seemed depressed. Like he knew that he'd be going back to Sly's kitchen soon. That the freedom he was given was fleeting faster and faster, and the inevitable was on its way to claim him once again.

"I think I'm just going to go to bed. Tomorrow we can explore, and I'll get some supplies for the kitchen," Jordon said as he placed **Chef's Kiss** on the table and stretched out on the couch. He started snoring within minutes.

I motioned for Paco to follow me outside so Jordon could sleep in peace. Paco nodded without saying a word.

"I figured he'd want to go see Wilduwen again," Paco said.

"Yeah, but this is probably the first time he hasn't been stressed since Sly abducted him. His body is crashing and trying to catch up on as much sleep as he can get. Who knows how little sleep he gets there. Sly could keep him up for days with whatever travelers come through that place."

"Hmmm. Yeah, I guess. But still, he should stay up a bit and just be outside."

"Tomorrow we can take him to the battlegrounds where we fought Squish. Maybe see how the dwarves are rebuilding the city. I'm sure it hasn't stopped since we left. It probably looks completely different," I said.

"What if Sly sends something else after us?"

I looked down at Paco and winked.

"I'm hoping he does."

Paco laughed. "Me, too. That stone golem wasn't that tough. Jordon took it out by himself and was a lower level. We can work on our fighting techniques and figure out how to work with Jordon so that when we get his contract, it'll be super easy for us to work together," Paco was excited as he spoke. I could tell that his imagination was running wild.

"I have an idea or two, but let's get some sleep. We'll have a full day with Jordon tomorrow."

"Okay," Paco replied as he ran for the door.

"Shhh, be quiet. I don't know how heavy of a sleeper he is. I don't want you making him mad most of all."

Paco opened the door and tiptoed to his sewer drain while waving to Jerry to follow him. He lifted the manhole cover and slowly lowered it back to the floor as he climbed down to his room.

Sleep took hold of me before a single thought could pass through my head.

I was sitting with my parents. It was Christmas morning, and the red wrapping paper of my gifts glistened in the lights underneath the tree. Our golden retriever was chewing on one of his toys.

"Go ahead, go open the big one," they said in unison.

I'm dreaming.

I crossed the room and pulled the large box out from underneath the tree. The paper tore with the distinct ripping sound of excitement that only a child knows.

Inside, there was a small gas-powered truck. I looked up to my parents and saw a flash of light. They screamed, but no sound came from their mouths. As I ran to the window, I could see the orc spaceships shooting down at the planet.

Each ship was green with large spikes. They all looked more like a magnet that had picked up too many nails from a construction site than an actual ship. The lasers continued to bombard Earth from the bellies of those ships. I blinked as one of the beams began to vaporize everything in front of the house.

I woke in a sweat to the sound of Paco and Jordon laughing.

"And then Chris started shooting all the arrows after he fell off of Squish," Paco said.

"Morning," I interjected.

"Morning," they said in unison.

"Didn't think I'd hear you both laughing together anytime soon."

"Paco was telling me how you almost pissed your pants when he made you climb into the cannon. Then you broke all your bones."

The memory of the pain I felt was still there, but my body had no soreness. I rubbed my right shoulder. "Yeah, I guess it's kinda funny now that it's over," I said. "So, what's the big plan for today?"

"Jordon wants to go see the goblin city. He said there may be some spices that the goblins had that he can bring back to Sly's. Maybe even cook us something before he goes."

"Sounds like a plan to me."

"Hey, you alright?" Jordon asked as I crossed the room and opened the door to the outside.

"Yeah, just a bad dream," I said as the sun beaming into my retinas reminded me of my parents screaming.

"Had plenty of those since Sly took me."

My life is a bad dream right now.

CHAPTER 29

22 HOURS REMAINING

JORDON HIT a home run on a bird that reminded me of a pterodactyl. It was only level 8, scrawny with wings that reminded me more of bones. Its body was off white and it had an elongated head that gave off a dinosaur aura. When it came screeching towards us, Jordon's ladle elongated almost immediately. He wound up and cracked it across the head so hard I thought he had decapitated the thing. The crunching sound brought flashbacks of Squish stomping down and pulverizing any dwarf or goblin beneath him. The bird went flying close to a hundred yards.

"Not bad," Jordon said as he slung the ladle onto his shoulder.

"Holy crap!" Paco ran up and put his paw to his brow. He tried to see how far the thing soared.

"Pretty sure it's dead," I said.

"Glad you're on our side," Paco said, looking up to the burly cook.

"I'm not on anyone's side. I'm just here," Jordon retorted. "Now let's get to that city," he pointed with the ladle. We walked around, spending our time talking rather than paying attention to our surroundings.

The wooden gate of Squish's city was fully restored. It had been lacquered to give off a nice mahogany shine that went well with the polished iron bars and studs that now adorned it. Each of the round towers had been fitted with huge balistas. The gate doors opened before we could even get close enough. Squish's body had already decomposed. All that was left were bones. I assumed Brukrag left them there as a threat to anyone who thought they could attack the city.

"Come," Brukrag said as he stood in the center.

No one said a word as we followed him up the stairs to the towers and stood directly above the gate. Jerry squealed as Paco lifted him. I couldn't see it from the battlefield, but there were four wooden carts loaded with at least two hundred arrows up here with us.

"What the hell are those?" I asked.

"Hwachas. Arrows with rockets on the back." Brukrag's voice was stern.

"You'll block out the sun if you get any more," Paco replied.

"That's the plan. Don't allow any infantry to come close to this place. Brukward and Brukhun are overseeing the construction of at least thirty-six more placed at equal intervals around the entire wall. Let the ballistas worry about any flyers that came to this place. Now, friends, why have you come here? Though I do enjoy your company, I figured your new friend here would want to see better things in this world than the reconstruction of a destroyed city." Brukrag turned around and walked to overlook the inner ward.

"It was my idea to come," Jordon said. "Wanted to see if there was anything here I could make use of before I went back to the kitchen."

"I doubt you'll find much. Goblins aren't known for their exquisite taste. They eat mostly oats boiled in the milk of a badger."

"Gross," Jordon said with clear disdain.

"As I said, not the most cultured. There wasn't much here that Squish hadn't taken for himself. Just some rusted-out knives we've been melting down," Brukrag shot Paco a look. "Which reminds me, what exactly did you loot from the goblin king's body?"

"Just some of the gems, gold, and his sword. I left the armor for you," Paco's voice was shaky.

"Ay, thank you for that. Lord Greatwood will have a monument made in his honor out of that gold," Brukrag said. There was a tone in his voice that I couldn't entirely place. Was it suspicion? Or was he hiding something from us that he had found here?

"Brukrag, I have a question," I interrupted them before Brukrag could ask to see the sword.

"What is it, Chris?"

"Obviously if we went towards the mountain, we'd find more goblins and demon hawks."

"Ay, and dragons, hobgoblins, elementals, cave badgers, and centaur aberrations."

"What's a centaur aberration?" Paco asked.

"Think of it like a horse, but there's a humanoid torso sewn onto its back that wails like a child in the night. The horse's head then sings, entrancing you to come slay the growth on its back. They work in unison throughout the song to lure dwarves and younglings to their death."

"That's fucking disgusting," Jordon replied.

"Okay, so what's the other way? What's away from the mountain? Further on from the starport?" I tried to bring the conversation back and pointed south.

"If you walk on for five days, you will reach the fey kingdom, and beyond that, you will reach the merfolk who reside in the waters."

"Are they friendly?" Paco asked.

"Neither is inherently friendly nor unfriendly. If you go as a visitor, the Fey will welcome you. The merfolk have built their city under the waves. Their visitors are few and far between."

"I see," Paco said.

Paco was interested in getting away from this place; I could tell. And it seemed to be a good idea for us to go explore this planet a bit, even if it was to make allies other than Brukrag.

"I think it's about time I get back to my work," Brukrag

said as he looked down on all the dwarves. They had built wooden cranes with ropes and pulleys. They hoisted large slabs of metal into the air. Every way you looked, they were placing something, hammering another, or cutting pieces of wood to exact measurements.

"With the blessing of Lord Greatwood, go in peace with the time you have left," Brukrag turned and put his arm on Jordon. He shrugged it off.

"I do not believe in your god," he replied.

"He is not a god, but one who has risen to ascension for the bravery he committed."

"Don't care," Jordon replied as he turned away and walked down the stairs.

"I'm sorry about him," I said.

"It is no matter. The abuse he suffers at the hands of that demon is bound to come out in ways he does not mean for."

I nodded and followed Jordon down to the courtyard and through the gates back to the battlefield. Now I was able to get a true look at it. The landscape had been pockmarked by explosions. Craters littered all around, and still, dead bodies were being cleaned up. All the dwarven bodies had been taken away, I noticed. All that remained were goblin limbs, and those who had rigor mortis set in.

"Jeez," Paco exclaimed.

"Yeah. Imagine seeing it with all the dead dwarves?"

"I don't even want to think about that," Paco replied.

"Doesn't matter, let's go," Jordon said.

"Are you ever just not an asshole?" I asked. Jordon's short

tone was becoming insufferable at this point. As much as Paco annoyed me, and our circumstances sucked, I didn't want to deal with the passive aggressiveness from someone else anymore.

"Nope," he replied.

"Come on, Paco. Pick up Jerry and let's go," I said as I walked in front. The little potbelly pig oinked as Paco lifted him from the ground. I heard Jordon walking behind us, but I didn't dare look back.

Overhead, the sun went dark. Not "covered by clouds" dark, but the world had gone black in an instant. I looked up.

It was unmistakable. I had seen it in my dream. There was an orc starship blanketing the sun. It was outlined in an eerie glow, like that of a solar eclipse. A door appeared in front of us and opened.

"Sssorry, cutting this ssshort. Time to go," Sly's voice came from inside as a huge hand made of smoke shot out of the doorway and pushed past me and Paco. We landed on our asses. Jerry squealed.

"No! Let me stay," Jordon shouted as the hand of smoke grabbed him. He was using the ladle to dig into the ground, but it was of no use. With one giant tug, he disappeared, ladle and all, into the void. The door slammed shut, then it disappeared.

New Quest.

Find the Hat Man (Step One)

Sorry, I hid this quest earlier. It's specific to you two. Jordon was a temporary party member. I could not assign this until after he left. Should he come back into the party,

you may still complete this quest. He will receive no loot or experience from it. Now, Brukrag warned you about the man in the hat. The man you see after taking too much flu medication. Find him. This is a multi-part quest.

"What's a hat man?"

"Who cares right now? The orcs are here!"

CHAPTER 30

THERE WAS a blast of blue light that shot down from the center of the ship. The ground illuminated as flames scorched the ground a few hundred feet in front of us. I could hear yelling coming from the city as horns blared. I turned to see the gates opening. Brukrag was leading the charge, this time without a mech. I felt the heat from the flames stop and turned back.

An orc stood where the blue fire scorched the earth. He had to be close to seven feet by my estimate. He wore a black cloak with a red clasp on it. He ran towards us.

"Battle positions," I said to Paco. He immediately jumped onto my back and handed me the chain. I wrapped it around my wrist and placed his favorite katana against the bowstring. He had cut a little notch in it for just this purpose.

"Who are you?" Paco shouted.

"I am Lieutenant Skarg, and I have been charged with

tracking down all refugees from Earth. Chris and Paco, you will return with me or die in the process," he grumbled as he closed the distance. His right hand was covered in a black armored gauntlet, which had spikes on it.

Lieutenant Skarg

Level 35

He likes to finish things up close and personal. His gauntlet will poison you. Do not get touched. Repeat, do not let the orc touch you.

"Now," Paco said as Skarg finally cleared one of the craters.

I loosed the katana. It cut through the air and stayed true. I tried my best to hold my pose so the chain wouldn't knock it off course.

Skarg raised his armored hand and batted the katana away like it was nothing. There was a metallic cracking sound that reverberated through the air as he did.

"Fuck," I muttered. I grabbed the chain and quickly dragged the sword back. I handed it to Paco. He held it in both his paws, hopped off my back, and stood next to me. We were ready for battle.

"We're really doing this?" he asked.

"I don't think we have a choice right now," I replied. I looked quickly over my shoulder to see Brukrag nearly beside us. "We have backup at least."

"Skarg does not like those who get involved in matters that are not their own," the orc said. He raised his arm and snapped. The gauntlet glowed bright blue as a bubble formed around us.

Trapped!

The enemy has set up a coliseum. Sorry. No one is coming to save you. Take his gauntlet, kill the orc, or die trying. That's the only way to clear it. No one gets in, no one gets out. Good luck. Rip and tear, little one.

You two need some battle music. Now playing "Paranoid" by Black Sabbath.

The fact that music was now blaring from my arm and Paco's leg pissed me off.

"We have no choice now," I said to Paco as I readied my bow.

"Then we fight," he replied. I watched him dig his feet into the ground. Jerry stood next to him, a fierce look on his face.

Skarg charged towards us. Paco did the same as I shot arrows as quickly as I could towards him. I saved all of my abilities for the moment. Jerry stayed next to me.

The orc repeatedly knocked my arrows away as they met in the middle.

"Okay," I sighed. "Time to do this the old-fashioned way." I put my bow on my back and pulled the battle ax from my inventory, and ran to catch up with Paco.

I was confident in my abilities as an archer, but Paco was erratic and liked to show off. I didn't want to hit him accidentally with one of my arrows while he jumped and danced around Skarg.

Paco hacked and slashed wildly at Skarg, who brushed off each attack like it was nothing. The clinging and clanging of metal on metal ricocheted off the barrier that surrounded us. I looked back and saw Brukrag beating on the force field. He was obviously yelling, but I could not hear a word.

Don't get any funny ideas. You can't message him either.

"Thanks for saving me the time."

I do what I can. Now go save the raccoon before he gets himself killed.

"How?" I asked as I was starting to breathe heavily.

I told you. Get the gauntlet. God, you humans really lack all comprehension, don't you?

I didn't reply. I was trying to figure out a way to get the gauntlet off his arm.

Paco jumped into the air and slashed down towards Skarg. The brutish orc grabbed him before the blade even came down. I heard Paco choking as he was dropped and punted towards me. He skidded and rolled in the dirt before he came to a stop at my feet.

"Give me the hamster," I said.

"Why?" Paco asked as he picked the katana up off the ground.

"We need to get the gauntlet off his arm. I have a stupid idea, but if you distract him, it might just work."

Paco nodded and unhooked the Hamster of Holding. He tossed it to me. It was heavier than I had expected.

"It has all my loot in it. Be careful," he said as he ran back towards Skarg.

I quickly looked through the hamster's inventory as I hooked it to my leather belt. Sure enough, everything was in there. All the items he had stolen, or body pieces he had cut off something.

CHAPTER 31

PACO TRIED A DIFFERENT TACTIC. He slowly walked around Skarg as I stood in front of him. The orc was uglier than I thought. His brow was huge, almost like a Neanderthal. He had no eyebrows. His canines bulged out of his mouth from the top and bottom. I could now see that the red sigil that kept his cloak together was actually a fist surrounded by blood splatter.

"Do you really think flanking me will work?" he grunted.

Neither of us responded. I ran forward, brandishing the ax, and swung for center mass. Paco ran and sliced towards the back of Skarg's knees.

We both watched as Skarg stepped towards the ax swing and punched the head of it. The dwarven ax exploded from the force. He then turned and kicked straight towards Paco's head. Paco saw it coming and turned his katana so it would stab through Skarg's foot. Skarg anticipated the movement.

He abruptly stopped, planted himself, and then punched down with his gauntlet.

Paco wasn't quick enough. The spiked fist connected and stunned Paco. I saw blood immediately start pouring from his face. He stumbled back and tried to wipe everything from pooling in his eyes.

"Chris, I can't heal. It says I've been **Plagued**," Paco yelled.

Plagued

Does not allow healing

Cooldown: 36 hours

"Shit, shit, shit!" I started digging through the hamster for anything I could use as a weapon as I tossed the wooden handle of the ax to the ground.

"Fuck it," I said as I turned back to look at Brukrag. He stood there looking defeated. I pulled Squish's sword from the hamster. I knew Brukrag could inspect it now, but I didn't care.

I ran forward and swung wildly. The sword was lighter than I expected it to be. I nicked Skarg's arm.

The orc looked at the green blood running down his arm, then at me.

"Interesting."

Buffed by Krik-krak

Strength +40

Bloodlust: activated

Immune to dwarves and dwarven weapons

Immune to elves and elvish weapons

Increased damage from dragons: 400%

Increased damage to enemies of goblins: 200%
Hidden

I could hear the sword whispering to me.

Feed. I must feed. Wielder, let me feed on the enemies of my kingdom.

"I didn't know you were enemies of goblins," I said to Skarg. I stepped around, wielding the sword in front of me.

"Of course we are. They are an abomination to this galaxy. Inferior in every way to the orcish race. When I'm done with you, I will destroy every last bastion of civilization. Our empire will spread throughout the universe and cleanse this place."

Skarg was too busy monologuing that he didn't hear Paco coming up behind him. He slashed and cut into the back of Skarg's legs, then quickly stepped back.

Skarg yelped in pain, then turned and swung his leg, narrowly missing Paco's head.

Paco ran around and stood next to me.

"You look good with a sword," he said. Blood still ran down his face, but it had slowed. In the distance, we saw another ship appear.

"They're back!" Paco pointed.

Skarg turned to look.

"Fools, you think those pathetic gray swine can save you?" He tightened his fist. The gauntlet glowed again, then he punched the air in front of him. Paco and I were hit with a concussive wave of air and flew back. My mouth filled with dirt.

Dizzy

I shook my head as I picked Squish's sword off the ground. The world was spinning, but not as bad as the demon hawk encounter. I ran forward and started slashing wildly at Skarg. He dodged or parried most of my swings. One connected to his gauntlet, but the sword did nothing to damage it.

"Paco, jump!" I shouted as I swung in a downward slash at the orc. Skarg grabbed it mid-swing as Paco ran up my back and launched himself into the air. He aimed his sword directly at Skarg's face. I felt a sharp pain in my stomach and found myself tumbling back as my breath escaped me. Skarg had kicked me right in the sternum. The sword clattered next to me.

Get up. Wielder, get up. I must feed.

"Do you want to quit?" I heard Skarg's voice. Paco was being held in the air. I watched as the raccoon struggled to free himself. He smashed his paws feebly into Skarg's forearm.

"Chris, help," he croaked. The orc smiled as he pulled his gauntlet back. The spikes grew larger, and he hit Paco directly in the jaw.

"No!" I shouted as Paco went limp. His jaw disconnected from his skull and splattered on the ground next to me. His tongue lolled around, and blood came like a waterfall from him. Skarg tossed him to the side. I watched Paco roll on the ground. His health back was blinking dangerously in the red.

I picked up the sword and unhooked the hamster.

"You're my best bet," I said to the furry creature I held in my hand. It blinked. I hoped it understood.

I ran towards Skarg and threw the hamster. It opened its mouth and engulfed the gauntlet.

"Yes!" I shouted as I slashed down on Skarg. The tip of the blade caught him in the shoulder as he stumbled back, trying to get the hamster off him.

"Nonsense," he muttered as he pulled the hamster off. I saw my opening and took it. I jumped and slashed down again. I severed Skarg's arm just above the elbow. The gauntlet and his lower arm fell to the ground with a thud.

I knew the shield fell away when I heard Brukrag shouting.

Skarg slammed the sigil on his chest, and the blue beam that came down splashed around him. He disappeared.

I picked up the hamster, grabbed the gauntlet with Skarg's arm still in it, and stowed the sword. Paco was lying motionless on the ground.

CHAPTER 32

"PACO..." my voice was low.

I bent down next to him. He was breathing, but it was shallow. His health bar was flashing. I picked him up and cradled him in my arms. I felt the warmth of his blood soaking my clothes.

"Give me the sword," Brukrag said as he ran up behind me. There was a small group of dwarves behind him. I noticed Brukward and Brukhun among them.

"Fuck off! Fix him!" I said as I turned, showing him what had happened to Paco.

"Chris, give me the sword," Brukrag said as he produced his ax.

"Cwris, it huwts," Paco tried to talk, but the words came out all wrong without the bottom part of his mouth.

"Shhhh, don't speak." I pulled up my inventory and equipped the sword. It appeared on my right hip.

"Give me the sword. I don't want to do this." Brukrag gripped his ax tight.

"Rip it from my cold, dead body," I said. The grays' spaceship moved across the sky and hovered above us.

"As you wish," Brukrag reached back and hacked down towards my head.

I curled Paco into the crook of my arm and extended my hand. I caught the shaft of the ax.

"How?"

My Strength stat was now over 50. I prayed that equipping the sword would give me that buff. I gambled correctly. I still heard the sword whispering to me. It told me to kill Brukrag.

I pulled the dwarf in closer. His ax rested on my shoulder. I moved my free hand to his forearm.

"Save the raccoon," I whispered.

"I can't," Brukrag said in return.

I felt warm. Buzzing. Like the world around me was lighter. It was the same sensation I had felt on Earth. I blinked.

We were on the grays' ship again. I was holding Brukrag's severed arm in my hand. His ax clattered to the floor.

"Give him to us," one of the grays said as they all ran to the platform I stood on.

I handed Paco over. He curled his tail up to his stomach as they rushed him away. I bent down and picked up Brukrag's ax. I put it in the hamster.

CHAPTER 33

I SAT in the command center of the ship. Grays walked by without paying me much notice. From what I could see, they were calculating where the orc ship had jumped to. There were lines on screens that had little dots across a star map, which connected everything. In the center of the room, there was a huge projection of the ship with letters in a language I couldn't understand. Even the AI attached to my arm didn't translate them for me. One of the doors opened, and Curly walked in. I could only tell because his name appeared above his head in blue writing.

"We've stopped the bleeding. The raccoon will live," he said as he came over and sat down next to me.

"Can you grow back his jaw?" I asked, wishing I had grabbed it off the ground. It was stupid, I knew. I had no idea that they would beam us up to the spaceship. I was prepared to fight Brukrag if I had to, but I really didn't want it to come to that. I'm sure he would be mad about his ax, which casually sat in the hamster attached to my waist.

"No. And we do not have any spare materials to make him a new one. Our resources are limited."

"What resources do you need?"

"We'd be able to mold him a new one and cybernetically attach it to his spinal cord and brain stem if we had plasteel or nuclear pasta."

"Would this work?" I asked as I took Squish's sword from my waistband and let it clang to the floor.

Curly looked at it, but did not touch it.

"It would, but those buffs and curses would be permanently attached to him. I do not recommend using that thing."

I sighed as I picked up the sword and shoved it down the hamster's gullet. I knew my next move was going to piss off Paco, but I had to do it.

"Take this then," I said as I shoved my hand into the wet mouth of the hamster. I pulled Brukrag's ax out and handed it over. The buffs were good, and I'm sure once Paco came to understand we couldn't use it to save Jordon, he'd appreciate it.

Ax of Lord Greatwood

Grants Ability: Power word

+10 Strength

+5 Intelligence

200% damage to goblins

200% damage to hobgoblins

50% to golems

Grants faster learning of spells

"You are sure?" Curly asked as he turned to me. His face was emotionless. I tried looking into the dark, bulbous eyes resting above the tiny mouth and below the massive forehead for any sign of what I should do. Curly did not give me anything to go on.

"I am," I said reluctantly.

"You will become an enemy of the dwarves…"

"I think I already am."

"It will be done," Curly replied as his four-fingered hand grabbed the ax from me and walked back through the doors.

I stood up and felt the exhaustion of the day taking hold of me.

"Oink."

"Wait, how did you get here?" I bent down and looked under my chair. Jerry was standing there looking up at me.

"We evacuated him after we beamed you guys up," one of the grays said.

"Thanks, I'm sure Paco will appreciate that."

"Go through that door there. You'll find your home just as you left it." He pointed to a door behind me. It was a standard bulkhead.

"How?"

"Safehouses are all connected, remember? Something the Council instituted for travelers. It requires a lot of inter-dimensional energy, but the Council provides."

I nodded and turned away. I vaguely remembered them explaining how these safe houses worked. I tried not to worry too much. Jerry followed me as we stepped through the massive metal doors. Inside, I found our living room. I sat on one of the couches. There was a piece of paper on the coffee table that I hadn't remembered being there.

Thanks for giving me some time away from Sly. Hopefully we find a way for me to get out of that hellhole. As much as he annoys me, I wanted to give him something in return.

I read the rest of the letter from Jordon. It was a recipe for Paco.

4 cans of San Marzano tomatoes

1 can of fire-roasted tomatoes

3-5 carrots

1-3 white onions

Shave carrots, cut in half.

Cut onions in half, peel off the outer layer.

Hand-crush San Marzano tomatoes, then mix in fire-roasted.

Coat the bottom of a saucepan with olive oil. Put in minced garlic, onions, and carrots. Turn to the lowest heat for 2-4 hours or until garlic starts to brown.

Dump in tomatoes. Keep on the lowest heat. Add salt, pepper, oregano, and thyme to taste.

Let sauce cook for 4-8 hours, stirring and tasting as you go.

Take out carrots.

Take out onions and save them for later. You can use them for sausage and peppers if you freeze the onions. Do whatever you want with the carrots. I hate them personally, but they stop the sauce from becoming too acidic.

Enjoy the sauce over pasta, with sausage and peppers, or home-made chunky pizza. Honestly, do whatever you want with it. Tell the raccoon I said "thanks."

"Damn," I said as I looked down at Jerry, who cocked his head. "I didn't expect him to just leave us a recipe to try. Don't know where I can get any of this shit though." I placed the recipe back on the table and relaxed back onto the couch. There was a squeak.

"Sorry," I said as I unhooked the hamster from my belt and held him in my hands. "You probably haven't stretched your legs at all since this started." I placed him on the table. "You did good today, too," I said.

The hamster started darting back and forth across the table as if he were looking for Paco.

"Me too," I said.

I watched the hamster eventually settle down on the piece of paper and then close his eyes.

CHAPTER 34

"WHO ARE YOU?" I asked as I stepped out of my room with Jerry in tow. I had slept almost twelve hours and was still rubbing the stiffness from my muscles from falling asleep sitting up on the couch.

"Officer RAT," he replied. He really was a rat. Full-grown, probably around five-foot-six. He wore a police badge and an all-black uniform. "Please just call me RAT."

"Okay, RAT. Where do you come from?" I walked into the command center and sat down in the same chair as yesterday.

"I am hired by the Council to provide protection for assets."

"Who is the asset? Me or the grays?"

"Both. The Council is currently working to revoke membership of the orcs, but legal battles ensue. I'm here to make sure that if there is an incursion, you are provided the best protection I can give."

"And if I don't want protection?"

"On this ship, you will have my protection. Off-ship? You may travel freely as you wish, though I would recommend you accept me as a party member."

"Pass," I said.

You should really reconsider. Paco almost died.

"No. Paco wouldn't want you as a party member, and I am not making that decision until he's here," I said.

"Fair enough, but on this ship, you will abide by the decision of the Council."

I scoffed in reply.

"What's so funny?" RAT asked.

"If the Council is that concerned about me, why aren't they here right now?"

"Though you and your race are of great concern to the Council, you are not *that* significant to them."

"Got it," I said as I stood up. Jerry stood up too. "Which way to food?" I asked one of the grays.

"Through that door," he pointed to the door Curly had walked through yesterday.

I didn't ask for permission to walk, just stepped away and continued through the corridors. I wasn't particularly hungry, but I didn't want to feel like I was being babysat by someone else. Someone I had just met. Brukrag was my babysitter, and look what happened there. He turned out to be in it for himself.

I found the cafeteria through the winding white and gray

corridors of the spaceship. After asking a few other grays who roamed randomly, I pulled up a chair in the center of the room. Jerry lay down on the floor next to me.

"What would you like?" a metallic voice from the ceiling asked me.

"I just want a black coffee, and a bacon, egg, and cheese on a roll. Salt, pepper, ketchup."

A circular tube snaked from the ceiling and created a vacuum noise as it connected to the table in front of me before pulling away. There was a steaming cup of coffee and the breakfast sandwich I asked for.

"Thank you," I said.

"My pleasure," the metallic voice replied.

I sat there slurping my coffee and eating my sandwich. The world around me felt like static as I disassociated from everyone who walked by. What had I gotten myself into? Maybe I should have just stayed in the town instead of poking around with Paco.

Jerry squealed. I looked down, and he was gone. I turned every which way as I felt my heart start to beat harder in my chest.

"Hi, Chris," Paco said behind me.

He was standing in the doorway. Both of his katanas were on his hip, and his armor was no longer covered in blood and dust.

"Come here, buddy," I said as I ran over and picked him up off the ground. I felt him nuzzle into the side of my neck. There was a coolness along with the warmth from his fur.

"Thank you," he whispered.

I pulled my head back and saw him up close. His lower jaw was now deep gray in color. There was a tooth that looked to be made of wood, and one of them glowed the same green as Brukrag's ax when it was used to power the mech.

"You're not mad?" I asked.

"I'm just disappointed. I wanted to use that ax to buy Jordon's contract. But, Curly let me know everything that happened. After Skarg punched me, everything went dark." His voice sounded deeper, and he spoke a little strangely. "They said it's going to take a bit to get used to," Paco said as he rubbed his new jaw.

"What's it like?"

"I can feel everything. They said there are nerves in it. A bunch of science-y stuff that I didn't understand. As my brain connects more with it, it'll be like it was naturally a part of me. There's also a chance my fur can grow from it, but I kinda don't want it to. I think I look cool."

"You sure do," I said as I carried him over to the table and placed him on the floor. He pulled out a chair and sat next to me. "I think you should take this back and thank him," I said as I handed the hamster back.

"What'd he do?" Paco asked as he stared at the hamster.

"He distracted Skarg long enough for me to cut his arm off. There's a gift in there for you."

Paco reached into the hamster and paused momentarily. He plucked out Skarg's arm and gauntlet, and then placed it on the table. He stared blankly at it.

"You okay?" I asked.

"Yeah. Yeah, I'm okay. It's just I never held something that almost killed me," he said. "It just feels weird. Wrong. I don't know how to describe it. It just feels empty inside me when I look at it."

"I get it," I said. "Let's put it away for now." I grabbed the gauntlet off the table and watched as the hamster opened its mouth. I stuffed it in there. The saliva that got on my hand was thick and slimy. I'd never get used to that.

"Want to go to the command center?" Paco asked.

"Yeah, grab Jerry."

Paco scooped the little pig up and carried him under his arm as we walked back through the corridor to the main hub of the gray's starship.

The main bulkhead opened, and we were greeted with confetti poppers. All the grays honked as we jumped at the sound.

"Welcome back," Curly said as he came up to see us. Ralph and John followed suit. Then the rest of the grays, whose names I never got, either shook our hands or high-fived us.

"Thank you, guys," Paco said. He was more reserved than usual.

"We're just glad you pulled through. Being **Plagued** is not an easy thing to come back from. We had to pump you full of potions to counteract it, then get your health up before we could do the surgery," Curly said.

"What do we do now?" I asked.

Curly looked over at me, then straightened himself.

"You are enemies of the Dwarven Empire. Not through

any fault of your own, but we cannot bring you back down to Brukrag. You will travel with us for the time being."

"And what happened to the orcs?" I followed up.

"They have cloaked themselves. We are tracking the signature of their stardrive in the region, but each time we pinpoint it, another pops up. There's not much else we know currently. I've decided that before we move to a different star system, we will stay here for the night. You guys need rest, and so do my people. They were all worried sick about you two."

I looked around at all the grays sitting at their stations. Their eyes were wider than usual. They all nodded as Curly spoke.

"I appreciate you guys saving us... twice."

"We do what we must. That's all we can ask of ourselves," Curly replied.

"Let's go get some rest then." I looked down at Paco, who was now carrying Jerry in his arms like a baby. I watched as he rubbed the tiny pig under the chin.

←Pointy
SkarG's
Gauntlet
I miss
my
saw...
Bil
PACO RACCOON!

CHAPTER 35

"YOU'RE LEVEL 27 NOW," I said to Paco who sat across from me.

"And you're level 29."

"I'm gonna do my stats, then go over some of my achievements."

We both sat on the couch applying everything.

Paco: Here you go

Strength: 19 (+10)

Dexterity: 12

Constitution: 24

Intelligence: 8 (+5)

Wisdom: 5

Charisma: 13

Chris: Here are mine.

Strength: 17

Dexterity: 28 (+6)

Constitution: 20 (+10)

Intelligence: 20

Wisdom: 5

Charisma: 5

(Hidden stat) Speed +4

"You put a lot into Constitution this time," I said.

"I don't want to die, Chris. Plus, my new jaw gives me a huge buff to Strength. I wanted to level up some other things. By the way, what is '**Power Word** '?"

"I'm honestly not too sure. None of the games I ever played used it."

Okay, nerds. Let me explain this the easy way. You use Power Word and say a word after it. Your enemy then does whatever that word is until it kills them—if it's effective against them. Bosses are generally immune. Some people are simple and say things like 'die,' or 'kill.' Others are a bit more creative in the ways they use it. There are some discrepancies in how it's exactly used, but that's how it works according to the Council.

"So, I can use **Power Word**—"

Careful. Don't cast it. You might kill the dumb human.

I gulped. Paco almost ended my life real quick.

"Got it. Okay. But, I can say that thing, activate the ability, and say something like 'piss,' and my enemy will pee until they dehydrate and die?" Paco asked.

"Jesus Christ, that sounds awful."

Yep. That's what would happen. Just don't cast it unless Chris has protection from it. Or you're out of range of other

party members. You might accidentally kill everything around you.

"Oh, I don't like that. I mean, it's good, but I don't wanna use it."

It scales with Intelligence. It is considered a spell, so congrats on your first spell, even if you stole it from someone.

The words stung Paco more than I expected. He really liked Brukrag, and to call him a thief for being saved by me just seemed like a low blow.

"Want to open our boxes?" I asked, trying to change the subject.

Paco had already started. I watched as three lootboxes appeared on the coffee table. There was a lot of fanfare and confetti popping out of them, which got Jerry pretty excited. He began bouncing up and down, oinking, and then running in circles. Paco threw him some food he had gotten from one of the lootboxes. The little pig ate it voraciously. I looked at my own screen and saw I had four achievements.

Achievement Unlocked

Save a party member from certain death. That should be glory enough, but I'll bite and let you have this lootbox.

It was a tiny wooden box. More like a trinket case to keep jewelry in. I opened it to find one gold coin.

"Fair enough."

Achievement Unlocked

Steal Brukrag's Ax. Unfortunately, you can no longer trade the ax for Jordon's contract.

Lootbox of the Thief

The box appeared, then poofed away in a cloud of smoke. On the table sat a contract that was stamped in big bold letters.

VOID.

"Okay, at least my boxes are useless," I said. Paco laughed.

Achievement Unlocked

Use an accessory as a weapon. Congrats. You used the hamster to win a fight. I actually haven't seen someone try to do that. Maybe next time you should have the hamster eat the orc and keep him locked away in the bowels of a rodent. Who am I to judge? Just food for thought.

The next box was the face of an orange hamster with white ears. I opened it. Inside, there was another hamster. This one had a little pink bow on it.

"*Oh!* You got your own Hamster of Holding. And it's a girl!" Paco pulled out his hamster and placed it on the table. There was a lot of squeaking as they ran off for what I could only assume to be some privacy.

"You can keep her if you want," I said to Paco.

"Really?"

"Yeah, I'm okay with my inventory right now."

Achievement Unlocked

Okay, this is kind of like a dual achievement just to save time. You've officially pissed off a lot of people. The orcs and the dwarves, mostly Brukrag, hate you. Wilduwen is probably still your friend, though I'm not too sure about Brukhun and Brukward. That being said, congratulations.

You defeated Skarg by yourself and pissed off a lot of people doing it.

The next lootbox appeared. This one had a name.

Mythril Lootbox of Failed Friendships.

I opened it. "Why Can't We Be Friends?" by WAR started playing.

I pulled an ax from the lootbox. It reminded me of Brukrag's, but didn't have any of the perks that Paco now had.

Stolen War-ax

Strength +5

200% Damage to goblins

200% Damage to hobgoblins

50% Damage to golems

"Why am I getting loot that I don't use?" I asked the AI.

Well, you did decide to steal an ax, and then you stole Brukrag's. It's only fitting that you get your own. Even if it was stolen from someone. But hey, at least this one is yours.

"All my loot sucks," I said to Paco. "What'd you get?"

"I got an achievement for almost dying…again. And a lootbox for changing a body part. Something about me being a 'cybernetic organism.' Then I got an achievement for keeping Jerry alive. That one just gave me food for him."

"What'd you get for the other two?"

"I got health potions, and one potion that if I drink it and take a mortal wound, I'll stay at one health."

"Okay, that's really good."

"Yeah, and then I got this metallic goop that I was told to rub on my sword." I watched as Paco pulled out his katana.

The handle was no longer wood. The name had changed again.

Satisfactory Stick of the Samurai

"Did it finally get some perks?" I asked.

"It did!"

Strength +1

Dexterity +1

5% Cooldown on Samurai abilities

"Good. That'll come in handy with your **Double Slash** and **Threaten**. Especially if it keeps reducing cooldowns."

"I want you to have something, Chris. I just need to find that hamster," Paco said as he got off the couch and followed the squeaking. He came back with one hamster on each hip. It was comical watching them try to swing themselves over to grab each other. Paco shoved his paw in the mouth of the male and pulled out the gauntlet.

"I don't want to hold on to this thing. And all your loot seems to be turning you into like an archer and melee build. It's better if you have it."

"I appreciate that," I said as I took the gauntlet from him. I didn't bother inspecting it. I had no plans of using it, at least not in the company of Paco. He was shaking like a leaf while he held it. I quickly put it into my inventory.

"I think I'm going to get some sleep."

"Me too. Tomorrow we're going to a new planet."

I watched as Jerry followed Paco to the manhole cover. He lifted it, scooped up Jerry, and climbed with one arm down the ladder.

Jerry
mohawk
tail
tiny feet
By PACO
KACLOON!

CHAPTER 36

PACO and I sat in the command center watching the grays walk back and forth.

"Who are you?" Paco asked.

"Officer RAT."

"I forgot to mention this," I told Paco.

"I am here on behalf of the Council. You will be under my protection as long as you are on this ship. Chris has already denied my joining the party."

Paco put out his paw and fist-bumped me.

"Yeah, no new party members for the time being. And you only protect us while we're on this ship?"

"That is correct. Once we get to our next destination, you will be free to roam within your party without my company."

"At least we have *some* freedom," Paco said. He had Jerry in his lap and kept stroking his mohawk. The little pig was growing tired. I watched his eyes close and reopen with each pet.

Curly walked into the room.

"Good morning. We will be jumping out of this quadrant shortly. From here, we will go to a world similar to your own. The population there is bipedal, though they look similar to what you call deer. Elkan is their official species name."

"How is the war going with the orcs?" I asked.

Curly let out a long breath and nodded his head as if he was about to break really bad news.

"Their citizenship in the Council has not been revoked. Earth is currently burning. There are pockets of civilization that are fighting back against the ground incursion. We have dropped supplies and weaponry down to the surface, but it's a bloody fight. The orcs have seen casualties, which is wonderful to see, but humanity is fighting a losing battle."

I started to space out as Curly continued to talk. The universe was heavy. Besides me and Jordon, I wasn't sure I'd ever see another person again. I'd always be a foreigner no matter where these guys took me.

"We'll figure something out," Paco said. "Find a way to take them on."

"It's not that easy," Curly said.

"It doesn't matter if it's easy. It matters if we do it," Paco shot back.

"There's a fire in you, little one. Depending on how your citizenship plays out, I'm sure someone will take you into their military with open arms."

"I'm not going anywhere without Chris."

Curly nodded and said nothing. He walked over to the Captain's chair in the center of the room and sat down. A steering wheel came out of the center console.

"Prepare the warp engines," he said.

The grays all started clicking away on their screens. There was a hum that began to fill the command center. The lights flickered, then shut off. The room was dark for a moment, and when the lights came back on. They were now scarlet.

Red Alert. Red Alert. Enemies on board. Prepare defenses. Red Alert. Red Alert. Enemies on board. Prepare defenses.

Curly shot up and ran to a screen. I didn't need to see what was on it. The orc starship had come into full view from the center window.

RAT ran to a closet and threw it open. grays lined up behind him as he began to toss silver and blue rifles to them.

"Line up! Pull that table out and leave the bulkheads open," he shouted to everyone. They took one of the tables and wedged it into the door before crouching behind it.

"You guys have guns?" Paco asked as he shot up, almost launching Jerry to the floor.

"Of course we have guns," RAT said back.

"I want a gun!"

"You are not authorized by the Council to use this technology. You will stand down and wait at the front of the Command Center."

"Oh, so if we get blasted, I'll just get sucked out into space. Great idea."

"The orcs are brash, but they aren't stupid. If they've sent a boarding party, the last thing they'll do is blow this ship up. The shields will hold."

I looked over to Curly for affirmation.

"The shields will hold," was all he said back before turning to the screens in front of him.

"Come on," I said as I placed my hand on Paco's back.

Before we could even turn away, I watched the doors down the corridor explode in a mess of orange flame and black smoke. Skarg stood there surrounded by orcs, who were all shorter than him. Where his arm once was, I could see an orange sword grafted to it.

Plasma Sword was all I could read before the grays started firing blue lasers from their guns. RAT jumped on the line and began laying down fire with everyone next to him.

I watched as Skarg ducked behind the destroyed door. Bolts of energy tore through his comrades, and I saw at least three fall where they stood.

"Get me another table!" RAT shouted to anyone.

One of the grays laid down his rifle and abandoned his post to pull another massive piece of metal to the defensive line.

"Cover me," RAT said as he stowed his rifle on his back. He kicked the legs off, then picked one up off the ground and shoved it through the center of the table. I watched as he picked it up by himself and placed it in the corridor.

"Holy shit, he's strong," I muttered.

"You two stay here!" he turned back to us. "Everyone else, follow me." He hopped over the barricade and grabbed the leg for leverage. He started moving forward as the grays followed behind him. They flanked each side as they slowly crept through the corridor towards Skarg. They all laid down covering fire as they pressed forward.

Curly stood with us.

"What is going on?" Paco asked.

"They want you dead for what you did to Skarg," he said flatly.

"What do we do?" I asked.

"Paco, sit here." Curly pulled out the chair he had once sat in. The steering wheel appeared. "You know how to use this?"

"Of course I do; it's just like the War Wagon."

"Good. Chris, you're over here with me."

We crossed the room and sat down. There were two joysticks on each side of the armrests.

"These are sensitive," Curly said.

"What do they do?"

Curly looked me dead in the eye. "They aim the lasers. When the white square on this screen turns red, you pull the trigger."

"You're fucking kidding me."

"No. I'm going to be on the torpedoes. I need you to blast their shields. If we can break them, I can get a lock and blow a hole clear through them. Paco, push the steering wheel in to go forward, pull it towards you to go in reverse. The bar at the top of your screen is power. Give us a go. But take it easy."

I felt the ship lurch forward, then the weight of the

universe started to crush my chest as Paco pushed his controls in way too far.

"Pull back! Too hard!" Curly shouted.

"Sorry! I'm not used to this."

I started maneuvering the lasers and got a lock on the orc ship. I pulled the triggers. The command center lit up in a brilliant light blue as I watched two beams shoot out from the front of the ship. They arced across the starship. When they cleared, I could see there was no damage done. Their shields had blocked everything.

"Good. Again," Curly said as he walked to another console and sat down.

A red blast covered the front of our ship.

"I thought you said they weren't going to shoot at us!" Paco shouted as he pulled back. I lurched forward, bumping my joysticks and shooting a wide arc over the enemy starship.

"Don't worry, just keep going. Rotate port side."

"What does that even mean!"

"Left! Go left!"

Paco twisted the wheel and pushed in more easily this time. The gray ship rotated and sped forward. I was barely pushed back in my chair. We were hit with another blast. This time it held for more than a few seconds.

"There's a flashing warning on my screen!"

"What does it say?" Curly asked without turning to look at Paco.

"Shields at fifty percent."

There was a guttural noise that came from Curly's mouth, which I could only assume was an expletive.

"Okay, aim towards Brukrag's homeworld. We might be able to go around them."

Paco twisted the steering wheel hard. I watched as the dwarven homeworld grew closer to us.

"Full speed ahead," Paco yelled.

"Incoming fire," Curly responded. The ship rumbled as we were hit by two red beams.

"Shields at critical," Paco announced. He turned to me with a scared look in his eyes. I focused on the screen and began returning blasts each time I got a lock.

As we started to orbit the planet, I could see the lasers arcing across the orc shields.

"Curly, if I don't have a lock, can I still fire?" I asked.

He gave me a look. One of doubt, desperation, or that I just shouldn't have asked.

"You can."

I looked at the screen, aimed the guns, and pulled the trigger after a few seconds. I timed it correctly.

The blue lasers burst forth and hit the orc ship directly as it came around the dwarven homeworld. Their shields stayed up, but I was confident that I had just scared the absolute shit out of them.

"Curly, fire the torpedoes."

"They won't do anything! Not with their shields up."

I fired another blast. "I don't care; we need to get away or we are well and truly fucked."

Curly looked at me, then nodded. He fired the torpedoes.

On the screen, I watched bay doors open. A mechanical arm dropped down, and eight long torpedoes sped through open space to their target. I fired again to try to take their shields down before the torpedoes hit. It didn't work.

The orcs had launched their own torpedoes and intercepted every one of ours. I watched as they all exploded in a massive fireball, which quickly dissipated. I wasn't sure how it worked in a vacuum, but I trusted my eyes. Maybe we were just close enough to the atmosphere of the planet.

Paco pushed as hard as he could into the steering wheel, and I was thrown into my chair. Two more red beams blasted us, then I felt our world rock as the lights flickered.

"Report!" Curly shouted.

"Shields are dead. And it says Critical Issue on the engines. I can't do anything! The steering wheel doesn't work," Paco was frantic as he stood up in his chair and looked back at us.

I felt the ship gliding slowly through space, then it became faster.

"We're being pulled in," Curly was solemn. "Paco, get on the steering wheel and face us towards the planet. I'm going to redirect power from non-essential rooms."

"What about everyone in there?" I asked.

Curly made a motion with his mouth. If he had been human, I would've assumed he bit his lip. I understood. He clicked away on his screen.

"I got some steering back. I can't do much."

"There's one engine with power. Just focus on facing us towards the planet. With any luck, you might save the day."

The words weighed heavily on Paco. There was a silence between us all as he robotically steered the ship. Then, I heard him start to cry.

"I never wanted this. I wish none of this was on me. Why did I have to live? Why didn't I just die on Earth?" Paco said.

The ship was turning towards the planet. I felt like the world was truly ending this time, and there was nothing we could do.

Curly got up and walked over to him. He placed one of his four-fingered hands on his back. A chair appeared from the floor, and Curly sat down.

"You owe a tremendous responsibility to the Milky Way right now. You are the only talking raccoon in your galaxy. It isn't fair, but it is what it is."

I watched as the world grew closer through the front windows.

"Do you not understand how beautiful and lonely you truly are? If you were to die or had been destroyed on Earth, no one would have ever perceived your galaxy or planet unless the Council came to visit. Do you get it now? You hold so much in your hands, and you wish that it were destroyed. What would the universe lose today if you were not able to perceive it?"

I could see the pinks of trees now.

Fire started to illuminate the front of the ship as everything began to rattle around us. Paco continued to cry and then yell as he tried to keep the ship straight. I got up and jumped behind the chair. Another had appeared from the floor, and I sat down. I wrapped my arms around Paco. If we died, at least we died together. He pulled hard as the continent came into view. My stomach was in my throat, which was also on the floor. We all screamed as the ship drew closer to the ground. Paco pulled as hard as he could, and the ship's nose lifted.

There was a crash that deafened the world.

Achievement Unlocked

The End

THANK YOU!

I hope you enjoyed this book. I fell in love with this genre as a reader and really enjoyed writing it. This is the part where I ask you to please leave a review. They truly help us indie authors. Feel free to find me on Booktok @nicholasturner-author. That's my handle pretty much everywhere.

I know readers of this genre like knowing how long a series is going to be. Upfront, I plan on Paco Saves the Day being four books. The next one already has a title: Paco Slays a Dragon!

A little side note for everyone wondering. Yes, I do love raccoons.

If you're new to my writing, RAT is based on a real person. My father passed away back in 2017 when I was 24. He always finds a way into my writing whether I mean to bring him up or not. His name was Richard Arthur Turner. I wanted to keep his memory alive, even if it meant I had to turn him into a RAT. I'm sure he would have hated it, then laughed about it. But, enough about me and grief.

I want to thank the following groups on Facebook and encourage you to join them. They allow us authors to post our books, come in and chat with readers, and spam them with whatever random ideas we have. Come in and get some awesome book recommendations. I love this community and want to watch it grow.

LitRPG Books

GameLitRPG Society

To learn more about LitRPG, talk to authors including myself, and just have an awesome time, please join the LitRPG Group

ALSO BY NICHOLAS TURNER

The Grid Series (Science fiction/Cyberpunk)

O Dreamer Mine (Science fiction/Horror)

I will also be posting Paco Slays a Dragon on my Patreon before it makes its way to RoyalRoad.

For $3 a month, you can get access to polls, ideas, and read it before anyone else.

Patreon.com/NicholasTurnerAuthor

I also write poetry under a pen-name: Nicholas Trieste.

If that's something that interests you, they can be found here.

Nicholas Trieste books